MW01133054

GETTING HOME

A POST-APOCALYPTIC EMP SURVIVAL THRILLER - THE EMP BOOK 7

RYAN WESTFIELD

1

DAN

"I'll be right back," said Dan.

The woman mumbled something unintelligible. Her hair was in her face, tangled and stained with her own blood. Blood ran down from her nose and into her mouth. The sleeve of her shirt was partially torn open, revealing the gunshot wound she'd received just minutes ago.

Leaving the wounded woman lying against the house, Dan rushed around to the back. The back door was locked. He considered trying to break it down, but it looked sturdily made, with a deadbolt. Dan wasn't big. He was just a kid, and much smaller than average.

How was he going to get inside the house?

He needed to do it soon. He needed to get himself and the woman out of view and into the relative safety of the home. They both needed to be out of sight. Dan didn't know where they were, and who was there.

Anyone could come by at any moment.

Dan's heart was pounding and his throat felt

constricted as he scanned the back of the house, looking
for a way in.

There was a window low enough for Dan to reach.

He had nothing with him. His knife was gone, as was
his pack.

Dan's eyes scanned the dingy back yard frantically,
looking for a rock. For something with enough heft
to work.

He was so anxious to get inside that he almost tried to
use his elbow. But he managed to stop himself. It was
likely it wouldn't work, and he'd just end up with an
injury that would hurt him down the line.

Surviving was a constant compromise between immediate and future needs. Sometimes, the immediate was
more important. Like when it was an obvious life or death
situation. Other times, like now, it was important to take a
mental step back and consider the outcomes.

There were no rocks visible in the yard. But there were
bricks that were half-buried in the ground, forming an
outline of what once might have been a small garden plot.

Dan quickly dug out one of the bricks. He didn't want
to injure his hand or wrist on the glass, so he took off his
shirt and wrapped it around his arm. Using the brick, he
smashed it against the glass window pane.

It shattered, leaving long fragments of glass trailing
out from the wood. It took just a few moments to knock
them away with the brick.

Dan dropped the brick, shook the glass out of his
shirt, then got it back on.

He was able to pull himself up and get through the
window without getting cut. He stepped down gingerly
onto the house's battered wooden floor. The shattered

window glass covered it, and it crunched underneath Dan's sneaker.

Dan suddenly realized that he'd assumed no one was home.

But he hadn't even knocked on the door to check.

Considering what he'd just been through, it was an understandable mistake. He was overwhelmed and scared and knew he needed to act fast. But whether it was understandable or not didn't matter.

If someone dangerous was in the house, he might die. He had nothing to defend himself with.

Dan stood perfectly still, painfully aware of how loud his breathing was. He waited and listened for any sounds.

But there was nothing. Not a single creak of the flooring. Not the faint hint of someone's breathing or movement.

Nothing.

Since the EMP, everything had gotten quieter. There wasn't that faint background noise from distant traffic that you never even noticed. There wasn't the sound of a heater or a water pump.

Nothing.

Dan had to get the woman inside the house. There wasn't time to check every room, to be absolutely certain that the house harbored no one.

He made his way into the kitchen, found the back door, and unlocked and unbolted it from the inside.

He found the thirtyish year old woman still slumped against the outside of the house, right where he'd left her.

"OK," said Dan. "We're going to get you inside. Don't worry. You holding up OK?"

The woman nodded vaguely.

She seemed to be getting worse.

"Can you answer me?" said Dan.

"...Yes," she said, after a long pause, blood from her nose entering her mouth as she opened it.

Dan and the woman had been lucky. The pickup truck driver hadn't spotted them jumping off. And none of the other soldiers had either.

Hopefully, the soldiers wouldn't know where Dan had jumped off. The route they'd followed was long. It'd be too hard for the soldiers to retrace and it and search each house along the way.

Dan and the woman should be safe from the soldiers in the house.

All he had to do was get her in there.

"All right," said Dan, crouching down. "I'm going to try to pick you up. OK?"

He didn't wait for her response.

He grabbed her under her armpits and pulled hard. He knew how to lift, to use his legs rather than his back.

It wasn't that she was heavy. She'd probably been an average weight for her height before the EMP, and since then she'd obviously lost weight. Just like most everyone else.

Dan was a strong kid. But he was just a kid. An unusually small short one at that.

He strained as he tried to pull her up.

He finally got her up into a standing position, back on her feet.

There was no way he could carry her inside.

"Can you walk if you put your weight on me?" said Dan.

"I think so," she said.

She leaned heavily on him, and Dan pushed back

against her with all his force. Like this, leaning crazily into each other, they managed to inch slowly step by step down the driveway to the back yard where the open door awaited them.

Somehow, Dan got her up the small concrete steps of the back stoop and inside to the kitchen where they both collapsed, exhausted, on the floor.

"OK," said Dan. "Don't worry. Everything's going to be OK. I'm going to get that bullet out of you. You're going to be fine."

But Dan didn't know that everything was going to be fine.

His eyes scanned the kitchen for something he could use.

He checked the drawers and cabinets, opening them frantically. He didn't bother looking for food and water. They'd have to worry about those sorts of supplies later.

Right now, he needed something to dig into the wound with, something to pull the bullet out with. He needed alcohol to sterilize the instrument with. And he'd need something to tie around the wound tightly, to stop the bleeding.

He wasn't expecting to find a full-fledged medical kit. On first impression, without careful inspection, it seemed as if whoever had lived in the house had abandoned it. If they'd had any time at all, they certainly would have taken with them whatever medical supplies they'd had.

If Dan hadn't lost his backpack, he'd be in much better shape.

But he had nothing.

There were some knives in the drawers. Regular dull kitchen knives, made of cheap steel.

He couldn't dig out a bullet with a knife.

Dan's eyes fell on an open door towards the end of the kitchen. It led to the dark basement below.

Maybe there'd be tools down there. Maybe pliers would work. He could sterilize the pliers as long as he had some alcohol.

It gave him a little hope, calming his mind a little.

"I'm going to head down to the basement," said Dan, crouching down to speak directly to the woman in a soft voice. "It's going to be OK. I'm going to get something that will help us get that bullet out of you. Don't worry."

Suddenly, there was a noise outside. From the back yard.

It wasn't loud. Dan wasn't even sure what it was, or if he'd really even heard it.

He and the woman both froze in place. Dan didn't move a muscle.

Then he heard it again.

It sounded like a footstep. Unmistakable. Dead leaves in the back yard crunching under a heavy foot.

Dan hadn't heard the sound of any vehicles. Hopefully it wasn't the soldiers who'd come back for them.

But who was it?

The best-case scenario was that it was someone inoffensive. Someone nonthreatening, nonviolent.

The chances of that were slim. And Dan knew that.

Dan's eyes skipped across the room, towards the drawer he'd just opened that had the kitchen knives.

It wouldn't be the first time he'd killed with a kitchen knife.

Another footstep. This one louder than the last one.

They were out of view for now.

But the window was broken, the cool air coming in. If

Dan got up, surely the approaching stranger would hear him.

He'd have to make it fast. Get the knife and be ready.

That was the plan.

2

J ames was exhausted. He stood there, leaning forward, hands on his knees. He gazed out at the bodies on the ground. They were in every pose imaginable. But most were lying face down in the dirt. There was blood on the ground and on the corpses.

"Come on, James," said his mother, speaking snappily. "We've got work to do."

James nodded.

They were trying to clear away the bodies from the campground.

There wasn't any hope in burying them. It'd be far too much work. Someone had suggested burning them on a massive funeral pyre, but of course that might attract unwanted attention. Their little daily campfire was risky enough. They didn't need to create a huge beacon that announced their presence.

The bodies might attract animals, but it still seemed like the best option. It wasn't like there were wolves in this part of the country.

Georgia reasoned that with the human population

dropping dramatically, the animal populations would start to surge. But that wouldn't happen overnight. Hopefully it'd be a happy problem for the human survivors, meaning more food for them, rather than more danger.

"Help me with this one here," said Georgia, pointing to a heavyset male corpse. His long hair was stained and matted with blood. He lay on his back. Bullets had opened up his chest. There were scratches all over his bare arms that his torn-up flannel shirt revealed. It seemed as if many of his injuries had been sustained before he came to the camp.

"You sure you can handle this, Mom?" said James. "I know you're feeling better, but shouldn't you take it easy? Especially with your back?"

"I'm fine," said Georgia as she crouched down and grabbed the corpse's ankles forcefully. "You take that end."

James knew better than to argue with his mother about her physical capabilities. And it did seem as if she'd improved dramatically. She almost seemed tougher than before, if that was even possible.

His hands gripping the corpse's filthy armpits, James groaned as he lifted him up on his mother's count of three.

"Faster than dragging him," muttered Georgia as they walked the corpse away from the campsite.

Nearby, John and Cynthia were doing the same thing. Sadie was the only who wasn't considered strong enough to carry the corpses. But Georgia wouldn't give her a free pass, despite having been carried away. Instead, Georgia set Sadie to work gathering anything useful she could find on the corpses.

"Right here's fine," said Georgia, abruptly letting go of the corpse, leaving James to carry all the weight.

He dropped it too, his burning, exhausted muscles feeling immediate release as the corpse fell heavily to the ground. There were at least ten other corpses nearby, hidden from the camp's view by only a couple trees. There were still five or so corpses near the camp that needed to be dragged away.

"Can't we get something to eat before we do the rest of them?" said James.

"OK," said Georgia. "Let everyone know. But we've got to make it quick. I want to get the rest of these corpses out of here before nightfall."

James made his way slowly back to the tent. He was practically dragging his feet with exhaustion. His idea was to get some of the venison out and lay it out for everyone. That way they wouldn't have to go to the trouble of sorting through it themselves.

But what James found, he wasn't expecting at all.

Part of the tent had been sliced open, leaving a huge gaping tear in one of the sides.

James drew his handgun. He didn't wait or call for help. He wanted to do this himself.

It wasn't likely there was someone inside, but he lead with his handgun, just to make sure.

It was empty. There was no one there.

But someone, or someones, had been there.

Everything in the tent had been kept as neatly as possible. Georgia and Max wouldn't have had it any other way.

But now, everything lay scattered about, as if a small tornado had passed through the tent and thrown every-thing every which way.

Of course, it hadn't been a tornado. It'd been the mob. Some of them must have run through the tent while James and everyone else had been fighting for their lives.

Clothes lay scattered on the ground, looking like they'd been trampled.

Replacing his gun in its holster, James bent down and started sorting through the possessions, looking for the food.

The venison they'd dried was completely gone. As were the cans of food from the pot farmers.

James's heart started pounding faster.

They'd survived the rush of the mob. But how long would they last if all their food was gone?

There was more food in the van.

James hurried off to check it.

He glanced over his shoulder as he left the tent. He didn't want to tell anyone else yet. There wasn't any point in worrying them unnecessarily. Everyone had already been through so much.

His sister, Sadie, was sitting on the ground, looking beyond exhausted. There were no tears on her face, but it looked like she'd been crying. Her hair was dirty and tangled, and James remembered how much attention she'd paid to it before the EMP, before all this had started.

John and Cynthia were bickering, anger on their faces, as they argued over the best way to move one of the corpses. They stood on opposite ends of the corpse, John at the head and Cynthia had the feet.

Georgia hadn't stopped to rest. Instead, she was regathering the woodpile for the fire.

The back doors to the van were hanging wide open.

James' first impression wasn't good.

Gear spilled out of the back of the van. Shirts and jackets lay trampled on the ground.

The food was gone. Completely.

The mob had been so crazed that James doubted they were capable of systematically searching through the group's possession and finding the food.

It hadn't been one of the crazed desperate people. It'd been someone with more of their faculties intact.

Someone who'd used the mob's attack as an opportunity to get what they'd wanted. And that meant that they'd been there, waiting and watching. For who knew how long.

They might still be out there. Whoever they were.

James gave up searching. He sat on the edge of the van's floor, his legs hanging out the back door.

It wasn't all their food. They'd kept some of the canned food in pits dug into the earth, and they'd kept some of the venison hanging from a tree.

But the majority of their food was gone.

Sure, they could hunt more deer. Provided the mob hadn't scared them all off. Provided someone else hadn't hunted them all. They hadn't seen a deer for some days now, which was unusual, considering they were in the state hunting grounds, known for their deer populations.

The loss of the canned goods, which were meant to be used as emergency food, was a huge loss.

James' mind was panicking, and he couldn't get himself to calm down. His thoughts were racing.

He didn't want to tell his mother what had happened. He didn't want the others to know, even though he knew he had to tell them. They'd all been through so much. This was just another blow, one that he, even though it was irrational, wanted to spare the others from.

"Let's get a move on it, James!" called out Georgia,

suddenly looking in his direction and seeing him just sitting there.

James knew it was time. He had to tell her. He took a deep breath and stood up.

Suddenly, a realization hit him.

There'd been a lot of food that'd been taken.

Too much for a single person.

So there were others out there. A group of them, and they were now well-fed.

The mob's attack might not have been the worst of it.

3

MAX

Half a day earlier, hidden behind the trees, Max and Mandy had watched as their flipped over pickup truck had burned. They'd lost the majority of their gear, which had been packed away in the bed of the truck.

They'd been lucky to be alive. The men who'd burned the truck hadn't gone looking for Max and Mandy. Max didn't know why. And it didn't matter.

They didn't have much with them. Max had a water bottle that was half full. Nothing else in the way of food. All the pemmican had been in the truck. Max was furious with himself for not carrying some in his pocket. He should have known better, considering what he'd been through in the past.

There wasn't any point in lamenting his past decisions, though. Not now. They needed to press on. They needed to keep going.

Max and Mandy had been walking for half a day. They'd been following a road that led north, according to their compass. It wasn't one that they remembered from the maps. They kept off to the side, staying behind the cover of the trees when possible.

Max had his Glock with him. And a couple spare clips. He'd lost his rifle. He had his knife in its sheath, his compass, his Vostok watch, a fire starter and some alcohol-soaked cotton balls. He had some caffeine pills with him. Just a couple.

Mandy had her rifle, her handgun, and her Mora knife. That was about it.

They didn't have any maps. They'd been burned up along with everything else.

"You doing OK?" said Max.

Mandy had stopped. She was breathing heavily. Her brow was sweaty despite the cool weather. Her hair was greasy and some of it stuck to her forehead.

"I'm fine," said Mandy, having difficulty getting the words out since she was so out of breath.

"Let's take a break," said Max. "We've been going too fast."

"No," said Mandy, waving her hand at him. "I'm fine. Really. We've got to keep going."

Max was having his own problems. His leg was still hurting intensely. Each new step seemed to make it worse. It was stiff and the muscles would occasionally spasm in rebellion against the work they were forced to do.

"You want me to carry the rifle?" said Max.

"It's fine," said Mandy. "I know your leg's bothering you."

Max hadn't thought that anyone else could notice. But he supposed he must have been limping notably.

He knew he was better with a handgun than Mandy

was. So he decided it'd be better if she had the rifle anyway.

Mandy had said she was fine to keep moving, but she gave no indication that she was ready to keep going. Instead, she remained in place, panting. Max decided to give her a couple minutes. He'd go when she was ready.

If something happened, if they had to fight, they had a better chance of surviving if they were as rested as possible.

It'd be a delicate balance. The faster they got back to camp, or found food, the less time they'd spend weak from near-starvation. But getting back quickly meant taking more risks.

Max didn't know how long it would take to walk back to camp. He could guess, based on the speed they'd driven at to get here, but there were so many other variables that it wasn't really worth it. A couple days, give or take, was the most likely, providing that they didn't come across any unforeseen circumstances.

And Max was sure they'd come across unforeseen circumstances.

What he did know was that they'd need to find a source of food. They couldn't make it all the way back on empty stomachs.

"Maybe we should try to find a vehicle," said Mandy, breaking the silence of Max's swirling thoughts.

"Too dangerous," said Max. "You saw what happened when we were in the truck. It's like being in a huge moving target. And for all we know, we were lucky. It could be worse on the way back."

"You're probably right," said Mandy. "So what are we going to do? Where are we going to get food?"

"Well, it's hard without really knowing where we are. We're just going to have to do the best we can."

"What does that mean?"

"I don't know," said Max. "A house with some food in it. A convenience store that hasn't been raided."

"We have to find a more populated area first," said Mandy. "There's nothing along this highway, from what I can tell. And as you're always telling me, a more populated area means more dangers."

Max nodded. "I still don't have a sense of what's happened to the populated areas. But my guess is they're less dangerous now than in the immediate aftermath of the EMP."

"Sounds like more of a hope than a guess."

"I don't hope," said Max. "That can get you killed."

Mandy laughed.

It was good to see her face light up for a brief moment, the exhaustion seeming to fade away completely.

It hadn't even been meant to be funny. Max had been completely serious.

But now he laughed too, laughed at the obstacles ahead that they faced, laughed at the apparent hopelessness of it all, at himself and his attitude and perseverance that had saved their lives too many times to count.

"Come on," said Mandy. "Let's go. I'm ready. Thanks for waiting for me."

"Hey, I needed the break too," said Max, even though it wasn't completely true.

They set off, Mandy leading the way and Max taking up the rear.

He kept his eyes peeled as they walked, making sure to not get stuck looking only at the ground, as people tend to do when they get fatigued.

Mandy had lost some weight like the rest of them, but she still looked great. Her jeans were dirty and torn, but they still showed off her figure, and Max had to make sure he didn't focus too much on her up ahead leading the way. It was certainly more of a magnet for his eyes than just the ground alone.

As they walked, the sky above grew cloudy as rain clouds blew in. The grayness didn't last long before it started raining. It was a light rain, but they still got wet and eventually soaked as they continued on.

No one drove down the highway. The only sounds were of the rain and the occasional bird. Not to mention their own footsteps.

Max checked his watch. It read four thirty, the arrow-shaped hour hand pointing between the indices and glowing ever so slightly. The watch had an automatic movement, the kind that all watches had run off of before the invention of the quartz timepiece. It didn't require electricity. But it also wasn't as accurate as a quartz.

Max had regulated his watch himself, getting the daily accuracy rate as good as he could get it. But the watch still gained about five seconds per day. And that was back when he'd had a desk job in an office.

The timekeeping of automatic movements were sometimes affected by how wound up the mainspring of the watch was. And since the watch was charged by movement, a more vigorous lifestyle would keep the watch at a fuller charge.

The Vostok movement was a classic Russian design. Tough and rugged. Able to take a beating, but not as precise as the Swiss-made watch movements.

For all Max knew, his new lifestyle was making his watch run as much as thirty seconds fast per day. He figured that his watch, at this point, might be as much as half an hour off.

There was an atlas back at camp. If he looked up the sunrise times, he'd be able to set the watch accurately again.

Provided he got back to camp alive.

It wasn't like the exact time mattered so much now, anyway. Although if he needed to use the watch as a compass, aligning the hour hand with the direction of the sun, it might mean seriously decreased directional accuracy.

They walked for another half an hour through the rain before they came to anything.

It was a rest stop on the other side of the highway.

Max and Mandy stood there, in the cover of the trees, quite far back from the highway itself. They were wet and cold, shivering in the rain.

"I still haven't gotten used to seeing a highway completely empty like that," said Mandy.

"Let's hope it stays that way," said Max. "Come on."

"We're going to go over there?"

Max nodded.

"What if there's someone inside?"

"There might be. But we're going to need the food if we want to keep going. I'd do it myself, but I'm going to need backup."

"The thought of going into that place creeps me out," said Mandy.

"It should do more than that," said Max. "You should be scared. We have no idea who could be inside."

"Thanks, Max," said Mandy, flashing him a wry grin. "You really know what to say to calm me down."

"This is one of those times where we don't want to calm down," said Max. "The adrenaline helps."

Max went first, leaving the trees and taking his first step onto the highway in some time. The pavement was wet and his boot sent standing water up his already-soaked pants.

4

JANET

J anet turned around only once as she ran. She didn't see Art get shot, but she saw his body on the ground.

She just turned back around and kept sprinting down the suburban road. Her muscles burned. They felt like they were filled with lead. But she kept going, her sneakers pounding against the pavement. Her arms pumped at her sides, her handgun clutched in one hand.

She heard the shouts behind her. And the gunshots.

But she just kept running. As fast as she could.

She knew they'd have no mercy with her. And why should they? She'd betrayed the only people alive who knew her name. The militia was her family, and she was leaving it.

She knew their tricks. She knew how they operated. After all, until moments ago, she'd been one of them.

When searching someone, the militia followed a protocol that Sarge had taught them. They were trained to pair up and spread out. If Janet got far enough away, she was likely to encounter two militia members rather than a larger group.

If she was worth searching for, that is. A lot of the times the militia preferred to save their time and manpower and just let people who didn't matter go free.

But that was only for those who weren't threats.

And Janet was certainly a threat.

She knew many of the safe houses, many of the hideouts. She even knew where Sarge was.

If a militia member disobeyed an order, he was rewarded with a severe beating. Or a bullet in the head, depending on Sarge's mood.

If a militia member obviously defected, like deserting the safe house, they got a bullet in the head. No discussion. No questions.

What Janet had done was worse. She'd freed a prisoner.

She was going to get more than a bullet in the head if they caught her.

They'd revel in torturing her, causing as much pain as possible.

But she wasn't going to let that happen.

Her mind was so set on killing Sarge that she knew she wouldn't and couldn't let anything come between herself and her goal.

Janet couldn't run anymore. Not at the pace she'd been going.

She ducked between two houses, sprinting down the shared driveway.

The homes were large and had been, before the EMP, coveted and expensive places to live.

No one lived there anymore. Janet knew because she'd been part of the raiding party on these particular homes not that long ago. She and ten others had entered every house on this block and shot the people who'd been in the houses. They'd murdered them in cold blood.

It'd been hard for Janet at first to kill. In her former life, before the EMP, she'd been a hairstylist. But that was all so far in the past now. When she occasionally thought back to her old life, something she normally avoided doing, her memories didn't even feel like her own. They felt more like some movie of a stranger.

Janet was hardened now. Countless kills had done that to her. She had to survive. She did what she had to do. No matter what. No matter who she had to kill. She'd killed women and children. She'd tortured men until they'd cried and screamed and begged to be killed. She'd pulled out eyeballs and disemboweled living men.

That was just life. Life in the militia.

If she was being honest with herself, the transition to a hardened killer hadn't even been that hard for her.

It had been for some of the men in the militia. Many of them hadn't been able to hack it. They'd tried to sneak away in the middle of the night. And they'd gotten shot for it.

A lot of the time, it'd been Janet who'd shot them.

But somehow, slowly, the hardened personality that she wore like armor had started to unravel. She began having dreams of what had been done to her family, what the militia was really responsible for.

So in a split second she'd decided to leave. To stop it all.

Her mind had gone right to Sarge.

She had to kill him.

But she had to get to him first.

Janet knew that she didn't have much time. Two

militia members would show up soon. It wouldn't take them long.

She needed to get into a position that would give her a slight strategic advantage. After all, she had a realistic understanding of her own abilities. She knew that she wasn't any better than the rest of the militia guys. In fact, she was probably a lot worse at many things than some of them.

She'd never handled a gun before the EMP. Never even seen one.

She had plenty of experience now, though.

The yards here were large. A large shed sat in the back corner of one.

It was common knowledge among the militia that people on the run tried to hide in sheds. They were convenient and often unlocked.

But they were death traps. A quick burst of gunfire through the flimsy wooden sides and everyone inside would get hit.

Janet ran over to the shed. She grabbed the handle and turned it, pulling the door open just a hair. Hopefully that'd be enough to convince them that she'd gone into the shed. She didn't want to make it too obvious.

It was night, but the moon was out and the sky was cloudless. They'd be able to notice the small detail, and she'd have enough light to shoot them by.

There was a gazebo made of ornately-carved wood in the center of the yard. Janet briefly considered trying to duck down in there. It'd be a good vantage point to the shed. Very close. But not enough cover.

Her eyes continued scanning the yard.

There wasn't much time.

There were some bushes that grew right up against

the house. Before the EMP, they'd been kept neatly trimmed, and they hadn't grown much over the winter months. But they'd have to work.

Janet ran over to them and managed to squeeze herself between the bushes and the stucco-like siding that covered the lower portion of the house. The thin branches broke as she pushed her body farther into the space. The branches scratched her face and poked her.

But she could deal with minor discomfort. Especially if it meant surviving.

They should be here any moment now.

She waited, staying as still as she could. Her breathing was heavy and she tried to control it. She didn't want them to hear her.

Heavy footsteps running down the driveway, the soles of boots slapping against the pavement.

They were here.

Janet held her breath. She wouldn't let any sounds give her away.

Hopefully the bushes and the cover of night would be enough. Hopefully her trick with the shed door hadn't been too subtle. Hopefully whoever showed up wouldn't be smart enough to realize that Janet was a militia member herself, that she knew where they normally looked.

Looking out through the tangle of the dense leaves and branches, Janet saw two figures moving through the dark yard. One had a shotgun and one had a handgun. That was standard practice when there weren't enough guns of the ideal type to go around. Pair a guy with a handgun with a guy with something bigger.

Janet had her own handgun pointed out through the

bushes. Thorns dug into her flesh but she ignored it. She knew she was bleeding and she didn't care.

Neither of the figures spoke. They were approaching the shed cautiously, walking slowly now.

Janet knew she had to wait just long enough. They needed to be past her, with their backs to her.

Janet couldn't hold her breath any longer. It happened all of a sudden. Her body suddenly cried out for air. She breathed in sharply and involuntarily. She'd been so caught up in the moment she hadn't allowed herself to feel the lack of oxygen.

"What was that?"

Janet recognized the voice. It was Sloane, a man with a woman's name for some reason that no one had ever figured out.

Janet didn't hesitate. She squeezed the trigger.

Sloane was a bastard. He'd stolen her food more than once. And he'd rubbed it in her face too, enjoying the fact that he was bigger than she was and could do what he wanted.

The recoil must have knocked a branch loose, because the next thing Janet knew, she couldn't see anything.

A shotgun blast rang out.

Janet wasn't hit. They must have aimed blindly in her direction. Whoever the partner was.

Pushing aside the branches, Janet saw Sloane's body lying on the ground. He didn't seem to be dead. His body was convulsing on the ground violently. His partner crouched next to him, holding the shotgun. He seemed unsure if he should fight or help Sloane, his injured partner.

Helping fellow militia members wasn't the norm. In fact, the rule that Sarge had drilled into their heads was that they were supposed to leave a fallen comrade no matter what. Under no circumstances were they to compromise their victory by trying to help one of their own.

It was a vicious, heartless policy, but it worked.

Punishment for disobeying was severe.

It'd been hammered so hard into Janet's head that she hadn't batted an eyelash at leaving the traitor Art there on the ground. And she also couldn't understand this soldier's actions. He was hesitating. It was strange. Weird. Unusual.

Janet felt a surge of anger, as if she hadn't fled the militia. As if she hadn't deserted her unit. What was this soldier playing at? Didn't he understand the rules?

She snapped out of it, suddenly remembering which side she was actually on.

Janet's finger was on the trigger, pulling. Almost at the catch point.

But then she recognized, in a split second, the other soldier.

It was Bobby McAdams. Maybe the only kind person in the entire regiment. Somehow he'd managed to straddle the line between vicious killer and caring person. He was always helping out his fellow soldiers, often incurring the wrath of Sarge because of it. He was notorious for being genuinely kind and helpful.

She couldn't kill McAdams, could she?

Not only that, but she shouldn't do it.

It was wrong.

Then again, the whole militia was wrong.

McAdams turned, the moonlight on his face. She saw his features clearly, the boyish charm that he carried, the baby fat that he never seemed to lose no matter how little he'd eaten. It was the first time she'd seen him without that lopsided grin he always seemed to carry with him as if it was his lucky charm.

He wasn't trying to kill her. He wasn't shooting at her.

But he wouldn't let her go. He had his orders. And he'd never let anyone go before. Sure, he'd help his fellow soldiers. But now Janet was no longer a soldier.

If she revealed herself, he'd shoot her.

So she had no choice.

She could spin it any way she wanted to herself.

Actions were more important than thoughts.

Janet squeezed the trigger. The gun recoiled.

It was a good shot. Right in the forehead. His body remained upright for a few moments before he fell face-forward onto the yard, making a dull thud.

Janet's ears rang from the gunshots.

She got up quickly and out from behind the bush. Her clothes and skin were torn up from the branches.

Sloane was still alive, lying on his back. Blood gurgled out of his mouth. His eyes moved, following Janet. His expression was strange. He looked emotionally hurt, as if she'd done something to hurt his feelings.

"Sorry, Bobby," muttered Janet, looking down at Bobby's body.

The gunshots would be heard by the next pair of soldiers. They'd be coming for her soon.

Sloane tried to speak, but nothing but unintelligible gurgling noises came out.

Janet had no words for Sloane. She grabbed his shotgun. The handle was slick with blood.

Janet took off running, checking over her shoulder for the next pair of soldiers that she knew would come. Because they always came.

5

DAN

an wasn't as ready as he'd thought he'd been.

The door burst open suddenly. The next thing Dan knew, before he could act, the muzzle of a gun was pointed in his face. He could see up into the darkness of the barrel, a tunnel that lead to nothing but death.

"Drop the knife," said a deep male voice.

Dan didn't have a choice. One false move and he'd be dead. He hadn't even seen the man's face, but he knew from the voice that he meant what he said.

Dan dropped the knife, letting his fingers relax and the knife clatter to the kitchen floor.

The woman let out a moan of concern.

"Neither of you move," said the man. With his foot, he kicked the door closed behind him.

The three of them were alone in the kitchen. A slight breeze blew in through the broken window.

"What are you doing here?" said the man. "Who are you with?"

Dan's mind was racing. His heart was pounding.

He'd survived so far by using his brain, avoiding danger. And also by fighting his way out. He'd stabbed how many men? Two. He couldn't quite remember. It was a blur. Probably some kind of protective measure his own mind was taking, not allowing himself to fully be cognizant of the violence he himself had committed.

Of course, he didn't regret it one bit. He'd done what he had to do.

Dan's gut feeling was that violence wasn't going to help him here. Not now. After all, what could he do?

What's more, his gut was telling him that this man was reasonable. And that was in spite of the gun in his face.

Dan decided his best course of action was cooperation.

"I'm trying to help my friend here," said Dan. "She's injured."

"I can see that. What happened to her?"

Dan paused, not knowing if he should be truthful about the soldiers.

But as he looked beyond the gun's muzzle, he saw the man's face coming into focus for the first time.

He was in his forties. He had dark, sunken eyes, but there was something about them that seemed... Dan wasn't sure what. Hopeful, maybe?

His beard and hair were long and dirty. His clothes were torn and filthy. He wore what looked like a backpack, similar to the one Dan had carried until he'd run into the soldiers.

This man didn't look like a soldier. He looked like a regular guy trying to survive the chaos of the EMP's aftermath.

At least that's what Dan hoped.

And of course that didn't make him honest or safe.

Dan took a deep breath. Then he spoke. And if he was going to tell the story, he figured he might as well go all in. His only choice was to trust. "We were kidnapped. I didn't know her before."

"Who kidnapped you?" interjected the man.

"Some soldiers. I don't know who they were. They killed my friend. They had..."

"Military trucks and gear?"

"Yeah," said Dan. "How did you know?"

"They've been the scourge of this area for the last month."

"Who are they?"

"That's a complicated question."

The man seemed willing to have a conversation, to discuss things. That was a good sign.

"Are you going to kill us?" said Dan.

As Dan waited for an answer, he was painfully aware of his pounding heart. He held his breath.

"No," said the man. "Unless you try something."

"What do you want?"

The man lowered his gun, and offered Dan a hand, helping him stand up.

"I'm doing what everyone's doing. Looking for food. Gear."

"Scavenging?"

"Yeah. I have to be careful. I've come across some bad people. Sounds like you have, too."

"Your name isn't Max, by any chance?" said Dan, wondering if it was at all possible that this man was the same one that he'd spoken to on the radio.

But the man shook his head. "Nope. Call me Rob."

"I'm Dan, and this..."

He suddenly realized he didn't know the woman's

name. And what was more, she was in need of medical attention.

"I don't know her name. But she needs help. I need to get the bullet out of her."

Rob crouched down in front of the woman and began examining her. He took a careful look at her bullet wound.

"Hmm," he said. "It doesn't look too bad. It didn't hit anything important. I think I can get it out."

"Are you a doctor?" said Dan.

Rob laughed. "Not even close. But I've had the unfortunate displeasure of doing a few of these."

The way Rob spoke sounded almost eloquent, completely belying his rough and dirty appearance. Dan wondered what he'd done before the EMP, but this wasn't the time to ask.

"Can you speak?" said Rob, addressing the woman.

She looked up at Rob, opening her eyes fully for the first time since they'd gotten into the house.

"I think so," she croaked.

"What hurts?"

"My ankle."

"Can you walk?"

She shook her head.

"She could barely make it in here," said Dan.

"And the soldiers? You said you escaped. Do they know you're here?"

"I don't think so. They kept driving."

"That's good. But we don't have much time."

"We don't? I thought we'd have to stay here for a while and hide out."

Rob shook his head as he removed his backpack, opened it up, and began digging through it. Dan saw that his fingers and hands were filthy, as if he'd been digging in the dirt.

"We don't want to stay here long," said Rob. "When I hit houses like this, I'm always quick. I've had too many run-ins already. I know better now."

"Is it the soldiers?"

"Nope. Just regular people. They're the most dangerous sometimes. You got lucky with me, kid. If someone else had showed up, well, let's just say it wouldn't have gone so well."

Rob had emptied half of his backpack onto the kitchen floor. There were plastic grocery bags filled with things. The pack stank like partially-rancid food.

Finally Rob found what he was looking for. A small Dopp kit made of a synthetic black material.

Next, he fished out a large bottle of vodka from his pack. He unscrewed the flimsy lid, and for a moment Dan thought that Rob wasn't who he'd seemed to be. He wanted to take a drink now?

But Rob just splashed the vodka on his hands and rubbed them together vigorously. He got most of the dirt off and then splashed a little more.

"Nice and clean," he muttered to himself as he unzipped the bag. The contents, unlike those of the backpack, were neatly organized. It was some kind of field medical kit, with nice-looking metal instruments that gleamed when the light hit them.

From his pocket, Rob shook out a couple pills into his palm.

"Now you're going to want to take these," he said to the woman. "They're time release, so you'd better chew them."

He fed them gently into the woman's mouth.

She chewed them slowly, a look of pain on her face.

Dan watched as Rob splashed vodka onto a clean-looking rag and wiped down a pair of steel forceps.

"Now this is the really unpleasant part," he said. "It's Dan, right?"

Dan nodded.

"Now, Dan, I'm going to need you to cut away the rest of this young woman's sleeve there. You'll find a pair of scissors in the medical kit."

Dan took the scissors and found that his hands were trembling. But he managed to cut the woman's sleeve entirely off, revealing her bare arm over which the blood was running.

"We'll deal with the bleeding after I get the bullet out. Now if you could be so kind as to wipe away some of this blood, I can better see what I'm doing."

Dan followed Rob's instructions and wiped down the area.

"Now you're going to have to trust me," said Rob, speaking to the woman in a soothing voice. "This is going to hurt, and I'm not a doctor. But I've done this before. And unfortunately in these present conditions this is probably the best medical attention you're going to receive." He turned to Dan. "Why don't you get her something to bite down on in case those pills haven't kicked in yet."

Dan found an old wooden spoon in one of the cabinets and placed it in the woman's mouth. Her eyes, now with constricted pupils, drifted sleepily over to Dan's face as she bit gently down onto the spoon's handle.

Dan gave her a look that tried to convey what he was feeling, that they had no better option than to trust Rob even though they'd just met him.

"This is going to hurt like hell," said Rob.

Dan watched as Rob used the sterilized forceps to dig into the woman's wound.

Dan held his breath. It seemed to go on forever.

Rob remained completely silent.

It was hurting the woman. When Dan glanced at her face, the pain was plastered all over it. The agony seemed to be growing on it. She was biting down forcibly on the wooden spoon. Dan worried it might break.

It had only been a minute, maybe two, when Dan heard a sound from the other side of the house.

Rob glanced at him, his eyes wide with surprise.

"Shit, they're here."

"Who?"

"Other scroungers."

"What do we do?"

"I might only have one chance at this. You've got to get this one, kid. There's a handgun in my pack. In the bottom."

Dan didn't bother questioning it. He knew he needed to act. It was all up to him.

Dan dug frantically in the backpack, tossing aside more plastic bags and gear until he came to a handgun.

"It's loaded. You know how to use it?"

"I know the theory."

"That'll have to be good enough. Don't hesitate to use it. And remember, shoot at the torso. It's the easiest target."

"What if they're someone who's not a threat? How will I know?"

"I've been hitting houses in this area for weeks now, kid, and I haven't met anyone except you two who are not a threat. Like I said, you got lucky with me. Real lucky."

Dan stood up, gun in hand, took one last look at Rob, who had his forceps deep in the woman's arm.

There was another crash at the front of the house. It sounded like someone was breaking down the front door, crashing through the wood.

Rob was concentrating so much on trying to get the slug that he didn't even look up.

It was all up to Dan.

He could do it. He'd been through so much already. What was one more encounter? One more danger?

6

"I don't know if we should do this, Max," said Mandy.

"What choice do we have? We're going to need food. We simply can't make it back without anything."

"But there will be something else. Somewhere else to get food."

"We don't know that," said Max.

"But we don't know there will be any food in here ether," said Mandy.

"Exactly," said Max. "To maximize our chances of finding food, we're going to have to hit every place we see. It's just simple statistics."

They were standing outside the highway rest stop. It was a large one, as they go. Probably run by the state and populated by small chain restaurants. From the looks of it, there was also a convenience store inside, the kind that you might find attached to a gas station.

There were no cars in the parking spots, or by the dozen or so gas pumps. No cars trailed down the highway.

There was no one in sight, and the breeze blew against Mandy's face and hair, taking individual strands and pushing them around in a chaotic way.

"There's no sign of anyone inside," said Max. He had his face pressed up against the glass of the door to see into the darkened interior.

"That doesn't mean anything, and you know it. Plus, can you really see anything in there anyway?"

"There are some skylights," said Max. "It's not that badly lit."

Mandy didn't know why, but she had a horrible feeling in her gut about this, about going inside. Maybe it was her body trying to tell her something, or maybe it was just regular nervousness.

Max was pulling his Glock from its holster, getting ready to go through the doors.

It must just be regular nerves. Mandy needed to calm down. There wasn't any reason this situation would be any more dangerous than any of the countless others they'd been through. And it wasn't like there was any reason that her gut feeling would be real. There wasn't any reason to pay attention to it. She needed to be logical about this.

"OK," said Mandy. "I'm ready."

She already had her handgun in hand. Her rifle was slung over her shoulder. She reached down and felt the handle of her knife, just for reassurance, and to make sure that it was within reach if she needed it, rather than tangled up in her shirt or belt.

"We've got to keep quiet when we're in there," said Max.

"Got it," said Mandy. "All right, enough waiting around. Let's do this."

Max went first. The door was unlocked and opened silently. Mandy followed through the vestibule and the next set of doors.

Max paused there, probably waiting for their eyes to adjust to the dimmer light.

He was right, there were skylights, but they didn't seem to let in as much light as they should, and without artificial lighting, the interior of the rest stop was quite dark compared to being outside.

They stood there for a couple long minutes. Mandy heard nothing except the pounding of her own heart. Neither one of them moved except to turn their heads to scan their surroundings.

They'd entered through a side entrance, near the restrooms. From where they stood, they could see the main seating area. All the tables and chairs were exactly where they should be, upright rather than tipped over.

There wasn't anything, really, that looked out of place or unusual. The storefronts of the chain restaurants had been shut with their metal grates. It was as if the employees had simply locked up like on any normal day and gone home.

That was a good sign. Maybe there was some food still left there, provided she and Max could get into the fast food restaurants.

Of course, most of the food would be rotten. But there'd have to be something that wasn't perishable, that would have lasted these long weeks and months since the EMP.

If Mandy had come here after closing time before the EMP, everything would have looked mostly the same. The only difference she could sense was the overwhelming stench of rotten food. Probably coming from the trash cans that hadn't been taken outside.

Mandy glanced at Max, but she didn't dare speak. And neither did he.

Mandy's own eyes were now getting more adjusted to the semi-darkness. She could see as well as she could outside.

Max held up his hand, signaling that they were going to move out. He pointed to indicate the direction, then moved his hand in a way that indicated that he wanted Mandy to follow at a short distance.

Max went first. He didn't go for the big seating area with tables. Instead, he went right to the closed bathroom doors. He put his ear against the door to the women's restroom, then the men's. He shook his head, letting Mandy know that he didn't hear anything.

Max pushed open the door, and Mandy waited for a moment before following him.

The strong smell of urine met her as soon as she stepped across the threshold. But it wasn't as bad as the smell of rotting food. It was just from some urine collected in the urinals that hadn't been flushed away.

Max checked each stall, leading with his Glock, pushing open the stall doors carefully and slowly.

Why was he bothering to check each stall? It didn't seem likely that someone would be hiding in there.

But Mandy knew better than to speak. If someone was there, it would give away their presence.

And Mandy trusted Max. He seemed to have an instinct for these sorts of things.

So she followed him into the women's restroom, where, again, there was no one.

Max led her back out into the main area, and together they checked everywhere they could.

There was no sign of anyone.

Finally, Max spoke.

"Looks like we're clear," he said.

"You really wanted to be sure," said Mandy.

Max just nodded. He was looking off in the direction of the convenience store, which, like the restaurants, had a metal grate closed down over the entrance.

"It looks like they just shut everything down for the day normally," said Max. "Our best bet is the convenience store there."

When they got up to the entrance, they could see clearly into the store.

"It's not fully stocked," said Mandy.

"No," said Max, who hadn't reholstered his Glock. "No, it's not."

Some of the refrigerator doors were open. Some were partially open.

The soda section was more than half-empty. There was a collection of empty soda bottles, some of them crumpled, on the floor nearby.

The candy sections were completely depleted, with candy wrappers littering the floor.

"I can't see the other aisles," said Mandy. "But there are plenty of wrappers there on the floor. Looks like someone's already taken everything."

"Maybe not everything," said Max. "But what's strange is that they didn't just take it. They ate it there."

"What does that mean?"

"Well, considering that the grate here is locked..." Max tugged on the grate to demonstrate that it was locked in place. "I'd guess that someone's been coming here periodically, unlocking this grate, having a small meal, and then re-locking the grate behind them."

"So it'd have to be an employee."

"Or someone with the key."

"You think they're here now?"

Max had already turned around, his eyes scanning the big wide open space before them. But there was nothing but the empty tables and chairs, the stinking trash cans, and the large fake potted plants.

"Doesn't seem like it," said Max. "No signs of anyone living here. That's why I wanted to check the bathrooms first."

Mandy nodded, not wanting to admit that she hadn't known why Max was checking the bathrooms.

"So what are we going to do? Get going?"

"The food's right there," said Max. "All we need is a bag of beef jerky or some chips, a couple sodas, and it should be enough to get us back to the farm, so long as we're careful with it."

"But how are we going to open the gate?"

"I'm going to shoot it," said Max.

"Shoot it? I thought that was just something people did in movies."

"Supposedly it works," said Max. "I've never tried it, but I saw it on one of those real-or-fake TV shows once. Someone was watching it at work in the breakroom."

Max hardly ever talked about his pre-EMP life, let alone work, and she was surprised to even hear him mention it.

"You'd better stand back," said Max.

Mandy got herself a good distance from the lock, as did Max himself. He took careful aim, and with a single shot, shot right through the lock.

The gunshot rang out through the entire interior. Mandy's ears were ringing.

"We're in luck," said Max, yanking on the grate and pulling it up and out of the floor.

Mandy's stomach was already rumbling, excited about the possibility of beef jerky, soda, and candy. But before Max even had the gate all the way up, Mandy spotted something off at the far end of the room.

It was a man, tall and lean, standing there. His hair was long and a wild-looking beard covered his face, seeming to meld seamlessly with his hair. His clothes were filthy. They were all black. Standard black work pants. His shirt had a collar and some logo printed above the breast pocket. It was an employee's shirt, a uniform.

The man held no weapon. He just stood there, with a blank look on his face, and a blank look in his eyes.

7

JOHN

It was a new day, but John had been up all night. He'd volunteered for the night shift. Cynthia had stayed up along with him, but they'd been at opposite ends of the camp, and had only reconvened once in a while to chat briefly about the situation.

Now the light was rising and Georgia had just woken up. Her children were still sleeping.

"Nothing last night?" said Georgia, already at work, poking and prodding the fire, trying to get it going again for the morning coffee.

"Nope," said John. "No sign of whoever it was who stole all our food."

"That's what I thought," said Georgia. "If they're the kind of people who act like that, like thieves in the night, I doubt they're ready for any kind of confrontation. They're probably more scared of us than we are of them."

"I don't know," said John. "Maybe they just saw it as an opportunity. You know, get what they needed with the least risk involved. And if that's the case, what happens when they get more desperate?"

"More desperate than they are now? How long as it been since the EMP?"

"You're saying that they're already as desperate as they can be, I guess," said John. "But I don't think so. It's hard to gauge how low a man can sink when things get bad."

"I'm not saying we shouldn't be careful," said Georgia. "We've got to be alert and vigilant. But there's also work to be done. We've got to get to it. We've got to work on our own survival. Our long-term plans. If we sit around waiting for them, and they never show, we'll be in a terrible position in a month."

John nodded. What she was saying made a lot of sense. "What did you have in mind?"

"Well, I'm off to go hunt. Before the deer go to sleep. I'll try again this evening."

"Are you serious?" said Cynthia, who had just walked up. "You're going to go out alone?"

Georgia nodded. "I'll be fine."

"What if something happens? What if you run across them?"

"It's happened before," said Georgia. "And it worked out fine in the end."

"But you're still recovering, Georgia. You've got to remember that you're not as strong as you were before."

Georgia gave a little laugh. "Don't worry about me, Cynthia. I'll be fine. And anyway, the more people I take with me, the more likely it is it'll just spook the deer. We've got to eat. Unless you have any other suggestions on how we're going to eat?"

"What about the squirrel and rabbit traps?"

"Nothing's turned up in them. And we need calories. Deer are bigger. That's the simple truth. Now while I'm gone, I need everyone to be working on the perimeter ditches."

"The perimeter ditches?" said John. This was the first mention he'd heard of them.

"Yeah," said Georgia, who was working on getting the pot balanced just the right way above the flame. "I must have thought of it while I was sleeping. Let's see what you think."

"Right," said John, nodding for her to go ahead. "And make sure you make enough coffee. I'm going to need a few cups."

"We don't have an unlimited supply of it," said Georgia.

"Trust me, I'm going to need it today if I'm going to be digging ditches after just a couple hours of sleep."

"Fair enough," said Georgia. "So here's the idea. We dig ditches all around the camp. Far enough away that we won't step in them ourselves. But close enough so that we won't have an impossible project of digging endlessly."

"Ditches?" said Cynthia. "But how's that going to help us? If I were attacking the camp, I'd just step over the ditches."

"We cover them up," said Georgia. "It's simple, really. All we have to do is make a grid out of some sticks. Brittle, thin sticks that'll break easily under any weight at all. But they'll be enough to cover with dead leaves."

"You think that'll work?" said John.

"If we camouflage it well enough," said Georgia. "Yeah, I think it will. We just need the ditches wide and deep enough that they're a serious problem when you fall into one."

"So it's basically like a long, extended animal trap,"

said John. "We could put sharp sticks in there, just like with the other traps."

"Yeah," said Georgia. "First we'll start with the ditches and see how that goes. My only worry is that one of us may fall into it accidentally."

"It'd probably be me," said Cynthia. "I'm usually the first one that that sort of thing happens to."

"Maybe we'd better hold off on the sharpened sticks for now, then, yeah," said John. "Well, after coffee I'll get to it. It's probably best to let James and Sadie sleep a little longer. They're pretty exhausted after yesterday."

"Nonsense," said Georgia. "They need to get moving. Sadie! James! Time to get up!"

"You really go too easy on them," said Cynthia, unable to hold back her sarcasm any longer.

Georgia just ignored her.

The coffee was ready and she poured herself a cup.

"Serve yourselves," she said. "I'm going to take off. Make sure James and Sadie don't sleep any longer."

"Will do," said John, reaching for the coffee.

He watched as Georgia downed her steaming black coffee in two long gulps. She got her rifle from where it leaned against the van, and she was off without even looking back.

"I hope she's OK," said John, as Georgia disappeared through the trees.

"I'd be more worried about whoever stumbles across her," said Cynthia.

James and Sadie were sleepily emerging from the tent and the van, rubbing their eyes, their hair a mess. Like the rest of them, they'd slept in their dirty clothes.

"We've got some coffee for you two," said John. "Your mom said to say good morning, but she's off hunting."

James gave a little laugh. "I don't think she's ever said good morning," he said. "It's more like 'get to work now, James.'"

"You holding up OK, Sadie?" said Cynthia, putting her arm around Sadie.

Sadie nodded. "I'm fine," she said.

"But you feel cold. Almost freezing. You're as cold as ice."

"Some coffee will warm her up," said John. "Here, let me get you a cup."

Coffee was the only thing the four of them had for breakfast. They didn't want to dip into the little food that they had left.

Cynthia, who'd been awake longer than John had, decided to take a nap for a couple hours. John, on the other hand, knew that he could push through for a day's worth of work.

They didn't have shovels, so they had to improvise. They spent some time finding pieces of wood that they could use. They worked on the wood, carving out flat shovel-like areas that would hopefully serve in the cold ground.

"Is this really going to work?" said James. "I mean, do you think it's going to be enough if the people who stole our food come back?"

"Let's hope so," said John. "It was your mom's idea. And she's pretty smart about this kind of stuff."

John had finished the last of the coffee, and he was starting to feel jittery and a little energized. Without any food in his stomach, he felt on edge. But that was OK, as long as he could get the work done.

"Let's hope your mom shoots a deer," said John as he

walked the perimeter of the camp with James and Sadie, making marks with sticks as to where the ditch would run.

"What if there aren't any?" said Sadie. "What if they all left? They might have gotten scared away by the mob."

"That's crazy, Sadie," said James. "This is their home. They're not just going to leave."

"What do you think, John?" said Sadie, who clearly wasn't buying what her brother was saying.

"I don't know, Sadie," said John, pushing another stick into the ground to serve as a marker. "I could see it going either way, honestly. We won't know until your mom comes back and tells us. Now let's get to digging."

The chatter quickly died away as they started to work. The sun rose slowly over them. The sky was cloudless, and the sun warmed them.

Soon John was sweating, and he took off the wool work shirt that he'd been wearing for days, tying it around his waist.

It was hard to dig with the sticks, but it was better than doing it with their hands. If they'd had shovels, the job would have been a long one, but with the sticks, it seemed almost like an impossible one.

John tried to keep his mind focused on the task at hand rather than worrying about how impossible it seemed to dig a perimeter ditch. When he couldn't simply think of digging and more digging, he tried to think of other ways that he could speed up the process. But nothing came to him.

What would Max have done if he'd been here? Would he have had some brilliant solution to the problem?

Probably not.

And that was just being realistic, discounting the problems that John and Max had had between them.

As far as John was concerned, that was just normal sibling stuff. Brother stuff.

But he did wish that Max hadn't taken off.

Who knew if he'd ever see him or Mandy again.

John and Cynthia had traveled so far and taken so many risks just to meet up with Max. And then what had Max done? He'd simply taken off on some new fool's errand, leaving everyone behind to fend for themselves. He hadn't been there when things had gotten really bad, when the mob had invaded.

And who knew how much time was left before another mob came through?

John's main hope, as terrible as it was, was that most everyone had, at this point, died off. That meant fewer threats and dangers for him and the group. Before reaching Max, John had been focused on just surviving from minute to minute.

Now that he was here, now that he had a camp and a group, his thoughts had turned more to the long-term. When he had time to think, that was, and when he wasn't too exhausted to think a single thought.

The way John saw it, the majority of the population dying off was only the beginning. After that, there'd be completely new challenges. Long-term survival was a completely different game.

Of course, there'd be an upside to that part of journey. They'd be able to conduct supply raids more easily and with less danger. They might be able to get a couple vehicles, a lot of gas, to make the trips easier. They wouldn't be able to expect to find anything perishable like food. But there'd be many leftovers of civilization that would aid them.

Some shovels from a big box store would be a great start.

"Shit," muttered John, as his stick broke in the dirt. He'd only managed to get about a foot down, and the hole he'd dug had a minuscule diameter. It wasn't looking anything like a ditch, let alone a ditch that completely encompassed the camp.

It seemed hopeless. The whole project.

By the looks of it, Sadie and James weren't having any luck either.

James was sweating and working up a storm. He was trying to get as much done as possible, digging frantically and at top speed, not accomplishing much at all.

"Take it easy, James," said John. "We don't want to tire ourselves out. We've got a long day of work in front of us."

He knew James was just trying his best, trying to protect his family. It was written all over his face.

John's eyes fell on Sadie, whose hole seemed somehow to be bigger than either his own or James's. There was a substantial pile of dirt next to her.

John stood up and walked over to Sadie in order to get a better look at what she was doing.

To John's surprise, she'd completely abandoned the carved stick. It lay in two pieces, broken, on the ground. Instead, she'd found a large flat rock.

"You might be smarter than all of us, Sadie," said John. "Looks like that rock's working really well."

Sadie just smiled shyly up at him. She seemed to be having a hard time getting over the events of yesterday. But she was working hard, and still thinking clearly. She'd get over it soon enough. They'd all been through horrible things. It was probably harder for her, since she was still a kid and her brain was still forming.

But in the end, maybe she'd grow up to be more prepared and better able to cope than any of the adults. In a few years, provided they were all still alive, Sadie would have essentially grown up in the new world, while the adults would have had to adapt more than she had.

Sadie showed James and John the type of stone that she was using, and she helped find them each one.

The stones worked better than the sticks, and John felt foolish for not thinking of something so simple sooner. But that was the way it was. He was hungry and tired and stressed, making for perfect conditions for less-than-optimal brain function.

The day wore slowly on, and soon John was too tired to think any thoughts at all. His hole got deeper and wider, and gradually he connected it to the holes that James and Sadie had done. The ditch was starting to form, and the task at hand no longer seemed so pointless.

Cynthia woke up after a few hours and sleepily began digging alongside them, gradually waking up as the sun continued to rise.

There was no sign of Georgia, but no one mentioned it. John got the sense that both Sadie and James were worried about their mom, but that the way they dealt with it was similar to the way that Georgia herself would have dealt with a similar situation, and that was just continuing at the task at hand, rather than wasting energy on something that they couldn't change. Georgia had taught them well.

All they could really do now was dig. And hope that no new enemies arrived while they were digging.

They all had their guns with them. John hadn't taken the rifle off his back, or his handgun from its holster, despite how uncomfortable it was to dig with them digging into him when he was down on his hands and his knees.

8

DAN

Dan approached the front door cautiously, working his way through the hallways lined with faded and ancient wallpaper that peeled at the edges.

He held the gun in hands that trembled no matter how much he tried to steady them.

The unnamed woman's screams ran through the house.

The sounds at the front door continued. Thumping and banging and the crashing of wood.

Dan was as nervous as he'd ever been. But he was keeping it together.

He knew what he had to do.

Point and shoot.

That was it.

It sounded simple. But there were so many potential complications.

What Dan was most worried about was the shooting. He couldn't take Rob at his word that whoever was breaking in was dangerous. And deserved to die.

Dan was fine with killing to defend himself. He'd done it before. And he'd do it again.

But those had been cases where his own life was clearly in danger.

This wasn't one of those cases, as far as he could tell.

After all, how could Rob possibly know that some stranger breaking into the house would kill them without hesitation? He simply couldn't know.

Dan was close now. He was standing in the dimly-lit hallway that ran adjacent to the dining room.

The dining room had one long wooden table, the kind that was made to look ornate but was actually quite cheap in construction. A glitzy chandelier hung overhead. For some reason, there weren't any chairs.

It didn't look like the room had gotten much use.

Two windows, covered in dusty ancient blinds, led to the front of the house.

Should he try to look through them?

It depended on how far the intruder had gotten through the door.

One final crash made up Dan's mind for him.

He heard the footsteps inside. As clear as day.

Whoever it was was inside.

Dan pressed his back flat up against the wall. He'd have better luck lying in wait than going to confront them, whoever they were.

The footsteps paused. No movement for a full minute.

Surely the intruder would hear the woman's screams. Another one, loud and vicious sounding, rang through the house yet again.

If it had been Dan, breaking into someone's house out of desperation, he'd have turned on his heel after hearing a scream like that.

But the footsteps continued. Whoever it was seemed intent on entering the house no matter what.

There was no telling how desperate they were.

Dan braced himself.

But it wasn't enough.

An adult man came crashing into the room, swinging a huge lamp right at Dan. Somehow he'd known where Dan had been. Maybe it'd been his shadow. Or a noise he made. Who knew. It wasn't like there was time to go back and mentally review the situation.

The lamp struck the gun Dan held and then smashed into his shoulder. Pain flared through him.

He didn't drop the gun. It was his lifeline. His only hope.

He couldn't overpower this huge man who towered over him, his eyes gleaming with anger and intensity.

The lamp dropped to the ground with a clatter.

The next thing Dan knew, the man had pinned his wrist against the wall. The handgun, which he gripped tightly, his finger on the trigger, was pointed uselessly at the ceiling.

The man brought up his knee swiftly. It smashed into Dan's stomach. The air rushed out of his lungs, leaving him gasping.

A punch connected with the side of his head.

But he didn't drop the gun.

It was all happening so fast.

Dan hadn't even really reacted.

Where was Rob? Would he come? Surely he'd heard the commotion.

But the woman's scream pierced the air again. Rob was probably deep in the middle of the ramshackle surgery.

Dan brought his knee up hard and fast. It connected with the man's groin.

The man let out a grunt of pain, momentarily releasing his grip on Dan's wrist.

Dan couldn't overpower him. He didn't stand a chance against an adult in hand-to-hand combat. But all he had to do was get the gun in the right position.

Dan brought the gun down as fast he could, trying to get it into position.

He saw the man's eyes following the gun.

The man, still groaning in pain, managed to reach out. His hand, formed into a fist, moved swiftly through the air in a backhanded motion. It collided with the hard metal of the gun.

Dan still gripped the gun.

Dan pulled the trigger.

He felt the gun recoil as his arm was thrust to the side.

The bullet lodged itself in the opposite wall, right in the middle of one of the wallpaper's many ornate roses.

He'd pulled the trigger a split second too late.

The next thing Dan knew, he'd been knocked to the floor. He hadn't even seen the blow coming at him.

The man was going for the gun with both hands. Dan was holding onto it with all his might.

It seemed like the end.

Dan punched up with his free hand, his fist closed tightly. It knocked hard into the man's jaw. But it wasn't enough. He barely flinched.

There were loud footsteps coming from somewhere.

Was it Rob?

A single shot rang out, echoing in Dan's ears.

The man on top of him suddenly fell limp. The two hands on Dan's gun moved no more.

The limp body fell heavily onto Dan. No longer supported at all, all the weight was on him.

Hot blood gushed onto Dan's face.

Still not releasing the gun, Dan pushed up, trying to get the limp body off of him.

"Just a second," came Rob's voice from above.

The next thing Dan knew, Rob was pulling the corpse off of him. He caught a glimpse of Rob's face finally, and he threw the body to the side, where it landed heavily on the thin wooden floorboards of the dining room.

Rob was standing there. He'd laid his gun on the dining room table. He fished into his pocket, pulled out a dirty white handkerchief, and handed it to Dan. "For the blood," he said. "Don't worry. It's about as clean as anything else we've got on hand."

Dan wiped the warm blood from his face as best he could. He could taste it in his mouth, as some had gotten in there. He spit on the floor a couple times, but the taste remained. For some reason, it tasted slightly metallic. Maybe something to do with the dead man's blood, some nutritional deficiency he was suffering from.

"How is she?" was the first thing that came out of Dan's mouth.

"She's fine. I finally got the bullet out. I would have come to help you sooner, but she was bleeding badly and I had to stop it."

Dan stood up slowly. From where he was, he could feel the air coming in through the busted front door.

"How many of these scrounger people are there?" said Dan. "You think anyone else will come by?"

"With the door broken like that? There'll definitely be more. We need to get out of here as soon as possible."

"I don't get it," said Dan. "This guy," gesturing to the

dead body, "heard her screaming, and still came in. He knew there were people in here. He wasn't even armed."

"They're desperate," said Rob. "Like the rest of us. But some are more desperate than the rest. This door is just going to be an invitation for those who can't even break down a door. Come on, you've got to help me with her."

"Did you get her name?" said Dan as he followed Rob, who toted his gun at his side, back into the kitchen.

"Her name? No. The pain pills kicked in and she's pretty loopy. You're going to have to help me get her out of here."

In the kitchen, the woman wasn't looking good. Most of the color had drained from her face. Her eyes were only partially open and her arm was covered in blood. But Rob had managed to bandage the wound in an almost professional-looking way. It looked clean, and the blood was only on the rest of the arm, not to mention the bottom of her shirt.

"She's going to be fine," said Rob. "But we're going to have to carry her out of here."

Dan didn't say it, but he was worried that he wouldn't be able to support her weight for very long, considering his small size. Even with Rob's help, Dan didn't know how far he could support her.

"Where are we going to go, though?"

"Anywhere that has an intact door," said Rob.

"Like next door?"

Rob, moving over to the window, pushed back the old curtains and peered out at the neighbor home, which couldn't have been more than twenty feet away.

"That'll have to work," he said.

Rob was quickly gathering up his things, shoving everything back into his bag. The only things that he took time with were his medical instruments, making sure that he wiped them down completely before replacing them in his little kit. "Never know when you're going to need these again," he remarked. "Better to take the time now, even though it doesn't appear that we have much of it. I don't think there's anything in this house worth taking. It's been hit before. So we'd better just move on out right now."

Together, Rob and Dan lifted the woman to her feet. She was groggy and could barely stand on her own. She groaned in pain whenever she accidentally put weight on her feet.

The three of them managed somehow to fit sideways in a line through the back door, back out the way that Dan had come in not that long ago.

Would the soldiers be looking for him? The thought crossed his mind as they stepped down the steps and outside once more, leaving the meager shelter of the house. He'd been convinced that they wouldn't be able to find him. But who knew?

It seemed like everyone was converging on him. It seemed as if he had no time left, as if everything was happening at exactly the worst possible time.

J anet was sprinting through the back yards.

She heard the gunshots before she saw the soldiers.

There were two figures, just outlines in the semi-darkness of the bright moonlight. They'd taken shelter behind the corner of a house up ahead.

She threw herself down onto the hard, cold ground. The gunfire continued, ringing out loudly.

She had no cover. There was nothing nearby that she could get to quickly enough.

Her only option was to return fire as quickly as she could, hoping that they didn't hit her in the process.

Fortunately, despite being in a militia, most of the members were bad shots. Some of them hadn't touched a gun before the EMP. Others, like the previously-incarcerated prisoners, had handled guns plenty of times before, but they'd never really developed any kind of proficiency with them.

They were the people who sometimes held handguns sideways, like they did in the movies, and really could barely aim. They'd brandished guns at bank tellers and shop clerks, occasionally shooting them. They weren't the types of people who went to the target range or practiced gun safety.

Janet squeezed the trigger. The shotgun kicked.

The figures were fully behind the house, taking cover, not knowing when the next blast would come. Good. That was the opportunity she needed.

She was up in a flash, sprinting, her arms pumping at her sides, her feet pounding into the grass. She got herself right up against the siding of the back of the house.

It would give her the benefit of surprise. They'd be looking for her where she'd been, in the middle of the yard.

There was a window about a foot away, leading right into the house.

More gunfire. One of the figures was leaning around the edge of the house.

Janet took careful aim, exhaling as she did, and pulled the trigger.

She felt the kick and her ears rang.

The figure up ahead looked like he'd been hit. Maybe partially. Or maybe not at all. He wasn't dead, since he'd gotten himself out of view again.

Janet took the butt of the shotgun and smashed it into the window. The glass broke, shattering, fragments falling into the house.

There wasn't time to worry about getting cut by the glass.

Janet lifted up her leg and stuck it through. A piece of glass cut her pants and dug into her. She ignored it, thrusting her whole body through. She had to squeeze in and position the shotgun just right.

The glass cut her face. Another piece cut her scalp. The blood was hot and poured down her face. But it wasn't serious.

What was serious was getting shot. Dying. She could deal with a little blood. A little glass.

She fell onto the floor. Hard.

She got up as quickly as she could. She knew they'd discover where she went.

There wasn't much time. She needed to get out of the house, making use of her small, brief advantage.

Her eyes briefly scanned the kitchen as she reloaded the shotgun.

It had once been a normal, if not quaint, kitchen, the type you'd find in almost any suburban home. The counters and cabinets weren't of the latest style. They were the ones you would have found in a home magazine a decade ago. But they still worked. Or had worked, served their purpose, before the EMP.

Janet didn't know what had happened here. But something had. The tables and chairs were overturned. The cupboards and drawers were all thrown open. Empty plastic bags of food littered the floor.

Blood stained one of the walls, and there was a trail of blood leading out of the room, as if a bleeding person, or a recently dead person, had been dragged from the room forcibly.

The room stank of old, rotten food, or stale, dead air.

Maybe Janet herself had come here once, on a raiding party. She didn't remember. There'd been so many of them.

She was already out of the kitchen and into the hall-way. It was dark, almost-pitch black. There weren't windows in the hallway, and not much light came through the windows anyway.

But she kept going forward, towards the front of the house. She didn't need to see. She knew where she had to go.

She didn't have much time. The soldiers would follow her through the broken glass. They'd be inside any moment. Or, if they were smart, they'd cut around to the front of the house.

Should she go back out the back? Should she wait, looking out the window, to see if they tried to come for her through the back? She could shoot them. She'd have the advantage, being inside the house.

No. She needed to press on. Get out of the house as quickly as possible. More soldiers might be coming.

She couldn't get stuck in this house. She wouldn't be able to fight her way out.

Suddenly, something slammed into the door. Loudly.

Shit.

Were they here already?

She heard another tremendous thud. Coming to her, in the pitch black hallway, it made her panic. Her heart started to pound.

She was losing her cool. Losing her bearings. The situation was too much for her.

No.

She could do this.

Another thud at the door. They were slamming something into the door, using something like an improvised battering ram. It seemed like the door was steel, judging from the way it was holding up and the sound.

They must have been different soldiers. There was no way the two that'd been shooting at her could have gotten there that fast. She'd barely been inside the house for a full minute, even though time felt like it had slowed down to the consistency of a thick sludge.

Janet slammed into something. She was moving so fast, and totally unable to see, that she'd crashed into a small wooden table, knocking it over completely. Her foot got tangled somehow in it, caught up in the thin spindly legs, and she fell over.

The shotgun clattered noisily to the wooden floor. Janet's head smashed into the edge of the knocked-over table.

Just then, the door burst open.

Janet hadn't realized how close she was to it. There must not have been any windows up there by the front door.

Moonlight crashed through, lighting up the area with that dim yellowish off-white light that seemed to make the whole scene more eerie.

A booted foot passed through the threshold of the doorway.

Janet was reaching for the shotgun. Her hand had been moving blindingly across the floor looking for it.

Her head was turned, looking for the gun. With the influx of moonlight, she saw it. Light glinted off the metal.

Her hand touched the metal, but no reassurance flowed through her. The blind panic, the clumsiness, though, did seem to fade. She was left with nothing but the cold knowledge of what she needed to do.

She raised the shotgun with her left hand, bringing it in front of her torso. Her other hand grabbed it.

A second boot crossed the threshold. The barrel of a shotgun was next.

As soon as the torso appeared, Janet pulled the trigger.

The shotgun kicked painfully into her breast. She hadn't had the time to get it positioned properly.

The figure was thrown back into the busted partially-opened door that had been knocked off its hinges. It hung there loosely until he slammed into it.

His chest was torn up from the shotgun blast, little pockets of blood on his filthy t-shirt.

She saw his face as he slid down, his legs giving out from under him. It wasn't anyone she recognized.

But she didn't breathe a sigh of relief. She was fine, at this point, killing those she knew, those that she'd lived with and fought with.

What sent a chill down her spine was the knowledge that another regiment had been dispatched.

There'd be... well, there wasn't any point in calculating the number... but it was a lot. A lot of soldiers who'd be hunting her down like a dog.

There was another soldier right before the threshold of the door. He was hanging back. He obviously knew that the second he stepped across, he'd be met with a blast from the shotgun.

Janet couldn't stay there forever.

She needed to get out.

She'd have to make the first move.

With her left hand, she seized one of the thin legs of the knocked-over table. She yanked it hard. The wood snapped.

She didn't waste a second. She scrambled to her feet, shotgun in one hand, the wooden leg in the other.

Quickly, she got close to the door. As close as she could without actually exposing her body to gunfire.

She tossed the wooden leg out the door, as hard as she

could, exposing her hand and arm only for the couple seconds that it took to toss it.

She didn't wait to hear what happened.

She lowered the shotgun, both hands on it, finger on the trigger, and stepped out in front of the busted and opened door.

She stood in a wide stance, legs spread, her feet around the half-dead man she'd just shot.

Throwing the wood had given her the split second that she needed. It had distracted him just enough to give her a slight advantage.

It was a duel. Whoever was faster would win.

Janet saw the whites of his eyes. She saw the surprise on his face. She saw the dawning realization that he was about to die.

She squeezed the trigger.

The shotgun kicked.

The soldier fell. It had been a good shot, catching him in the head and the neck. Close range. He was done for.

She didn't bother looking at the destruction she'd caused.

Underneath her, she heard the moaning of the half-dead man.

She heard movement. Something scraping.

Janet looked down. The soldier had taken a knife, and he was waving it around pathetically in the air, trying to slice Janet's ankles or legs.

Flipping the shotgun around, Janet slammed the butt of it into the man's face as hard as she could. It made a sickening sound.

The pain must have been too much for him. His hand seemed to go limp, and his grip on the knife fell away. Janet reached down and took it from him easily.

She said nothing as she ran the knife across his throat in one single quick and effective slice.

The blood gushed out.

Janet dropped the knife. She already had one.

The whole fight had taken only a couple minutes. It had felt like an eternity, but now that she was out of the thick of it, she realized just how little time had passed.

Those two other soldiers would have heard the gunshots. They'd be here any moment now.

Or maybe they were waiting for her outside, having gotten into some unassailable position.

What should she do?

Rushing out into the street, through the front door, meant certain death. If it wasn't the next two soldiers that killed her, it'd be the next two, or the next two. And that was if she was lucky.

She knew she'd already been lucky. Sure, she might have been smarter than the rest of them. Maybe her reflexes were better. But her luck wouldn't run forever. There was a practical limit to it. And that limit was death.

The tall man stood there with a blank expression on his face.

"Hands in the air," shouted Max, aiming his Glock, finger on the trigger.

The man did as he was asked. Slowly, he raised his hands above his head. The man had lost a lot of weight. His shirt hung strangely and loosely around him. With his arms in the air, the sleeves of the shirt fell away, revealing how emaciated his biceps had become.

His arms were like sticks, with the elbow the widest part of the arm.

"Don't move," shouted Max.

Max moved forward, and Mandy followed.

"Pat him down," said Max, standing about ten feet from the man, the Glock pointed right at his face. "One false move and you're dead. You try to hurt her, and you get a bullet. You understand?"

The man nodded. There wasn't fear in his eyes. There was nothing. Blank, wide eyes that said nothing at all.

Mandy patted him down quickly, doing a thorough

job.

"He's clean," she said. "No weapons. Nothing at all."

"Who doesn't have a weapon these days?" said Max.

The man didn't answer.

"Tell us what's going on," said Max, nodding to the Glock as an incentive. "How many of you are there here?"

The man began to speak in a halting voice, as if he wasn't used to speaking. "About twenty... no, I mean ten... of us."

"Which is it?"

"Ten, now."

"What happened to the rest?"

"Something bad."

Max interpreted that to mean they'd been killed.

Either the man was dumb, or he'd been through something horrible that had knocked a part of him loose, in some sense. But starvation alone was enough to do that to a man. It shouldn't have surprised Max.

"Do you have the key to the convenience store? Is that how you've been living? Eating the food there?"

The man nodded. "The key's around my neck."

"I must have missed it," said Mandy, reaching down under the man's chin and grabbing a lanyard. When she pulled it up, there was a cluster of a couple keys.

"So there are ten of you here? Living in the back or something?"

The man nodded slowly.

"Where?" said Max.

"In the backrooms."

"Are you all employees of this place?"

The man nodded. "A couple janitors... the employ-ees... most of us stayed here... the bus never came to pick us up."

"Show us," said Max.

Mandy sidled up next to Max, and whispered in his ear. "What do you want to see back there? We need to get moving."

"It's just a gut feeling," said Max. "I don't think there's much risk, and plus, we'll learn something."

"We'd better grab the food while we can," whispered Mandy. "If there's anything I've learned, it's that we've got to take what we can while we can. Five minutes in the backroom and that food might be gone."

"Good point," said Max. "You keep guard on this guy here. Keep your gun on him in case he tries anything."

Max didn't think the guy was a threat, but he'd gotten to the point that he didn't trust strangers. And he had good reason to be that way.

As Max hurried back to the convenience store, he thought back to their initial visit to the compound. Maybe Max had been suspicious there and hadn't followed his gut instinct, or maybe he'd been naïve and not been suspicious enough. Either way, what had seemed like an ideal rest during one of the hardest parts of their journey had quickly turned into a nightmare situation.

They'd made it out of the compound alive. Most of them, that is. Chad had lost his life.

Max had barely thought about Chad since it had happened. That was the way he was. He preferred to look to the future rather than the past. It was probably part of what had kept him alive so far.

But for some reason, he thought about him now.

Maybe the employee with the dead, blank eyes reminded him of Chad.

Now that he thought about it, there was something

strangely similar about them. What did that mean? Was the emaciated former employee also on opiates?

It was something to consider.

But it'd be strange if he'd had such a long-lasting supply.

What would Chad have done as the days gradually wore on and he eventually ran out of his drugs? It had seemed at first as if Chad could handle being clean. But he couldn't. It'd been too much for him.

Chad had gone out as best he could. He'd saved James's life in the process.

Max didn't judge Chad. There wasn't any point in deciding whether his actions had been right or wrong. None of that mattered. All that mattered was that Chad was dead and Max was alive.

There wasn't anything to learn from Chad. Max had never been tempted to go down that particular blind alley himself.

In the convenience store, Max found a couple of empty plastic bags behind the register and began stuffing them with bottles of warm soda, beef jerky and candy. There was still an ample supply of food in the convenience store.

Max wouldn't have thought that there'd be enough food here to feed ten people for such a long period of time. Maybe they'd been eating food from the other restaurants as well, supplementing their diets with the food from here.

What didn't make sense was how skinny the former employee was. It'd take very strong willpower to deny oneself the available food when the stomach was rumbling and the body was crying out for food. And that guy didn't seem like he had any willpower at all.

A brief pang of guilt flashed through Max.

Here he was, stealing food that belonged to others.

Was it right?

Max didn't know.

He pushed the thought out of his head.

He wasn't taking everything. Just enough for he and Mandy to get back safely to camp.

Max shut the gate as he left. It slammed into the floor, bouncing up a little.

"He didn't move," said Mandy, as Max approached them. "I think he's on something."

"Funny," said Max. "I was thinking the same thing."

The two of them waited, but the man said nothing.

"You on something?" said Max.

The man just smiled and nodded.

"Where are you getting it from, whatever it is?"

Mandy glanced over at Max. He knew she was probably thinking that if there was a supply of opiates, they should do what they could to get some of them. They'd be invaluable in the future for pain relief for serious injuries.

"All right," said Max, handing one of the plastic bags to Mandy so she could carry it. "Show us these backrooms where you're all living."

The man turned dumbly around and started leading the way.

"You sure this is safe?" whispered Mandy.

"No," said Max. "Keep your gun out, obviously. But if the rest of them are anything like this guy, they're not going to be much of a threat."

The former employee led them through big double doors that he unlocked, down a darkened hallway into the back rooms where the food deliveries had arrived.

There were no skylights here, and it was much, much

darker. A couple candles burned here and there, casting some dim light around. Some light came in from under the closed cargo doors.

The room was large, with a concrete floor. There were wooden pallets stacked here and there, along with some barrels of some unidentified substance.

The whole area stank. The inhabitants might have been defecating and urinating right there in the large room, rather than going outside. It would explain the stench.

But there was also the stench of rotten food.

"What's your name, anyway?" said Mandy, tugging on the arm of their guide.

"Jones," he said, speaking vaguely in that sleepy way.

"Why don't you introduce us to some of your friends, Jones," said Max.

"All righty," said Jones.

Jones led them through the maze of wooden pallets.

There were people scattered here and there on the floor. The majority of them were lying down. Some were on the wooden pallets. Some lay on the concrete floor. Some lay on piles of plastic bags and other strange things that they had gathered in order to form nest-like sleeping spots.

Some of the people snored loudly. Others seemed to be in a dream-like state, with their eyes half open, existing somewhere between dreams and reality.

Hardly anyone reacted to Max and Mandy's presence. Some of them gazed up at them with their strange blank eyes. But most of them didn't react at all, as if they weren't aware of anything.

"What the hell's going on with them?" said Mandy, not

bothering to whisper because it didn't seem like anyone was aware of what they were saying.

Max watched as Jones shuffled on over to a wooden pallet, and lay down on his back, staring at the ceiling. Apparently his duties as tour guide were over.

And apparently he wasn't concerned in the least bit that Max and Mandy had stolen some of his food, or that they had guns and had entered his safe haven.

"OK," said Mandy. "This is getting creepy. What the hell's going on here?"

Before Max could say anything, the sound of engines outside came drifting in through the cargo doors.

"I think we're about to get our answer," said Max. "Come on, we've got to hide."

Max and Mandy dashed off behind a big stack of cardboard boxes.

"Shouldn't we get out of here?" whispered Mandy.

There wasn't time.

Before they could even think about getting completely out of the room, one of the cargo doors opened up, making a metal-on-metal grinding noise as it did.

"Can you see anything?" whispered Mandy.

Max shook his head, and put his finger to his lips, signaling that they needed to be quiet.

Max set the plastic bag of food down on the ground, careful not to let it make any noise at all. He held his Glock, finger on the trigger.

He was ready.

He glanced at Mandy. She was breathing heavily, but she had determination in her eyes.

Whatever was about to happen, they'd be ready. They'd fight their way out if they had to. Whatever it took.

11

DAN

Dan and Rob had practically carried the woman across the driveway into the next house. There, Rob had picked the lock of the back door with a lock pick kit that he kept in a slender case in his front pocket. "Always handy to have," he'd muttered, slinging the kit back into his pocket, the door opening easily.

After checking the house to make sure there was no one there, Dan and Rob had gotten the woman situated in the living room. They'd set her down on the couch, trying to make her as comfortable as possible. She promptly went to sleep.

"She needs the rest," said Rob. "Getting a bullet removed is a lot for the body to go through, even though it was about as good as a gunshot can be, with the bullet lodged in there, that is."

"Couldn't be as bad as actually getting shot," said Dan.

"Good point," said Rob, settling down into a rocking chair.

The living room appeared to be completely undisturbed. There was no sign of anything having happened there. No furniture was overturned, and nothing appeared to be missing.

In fact, if it hadn't been for the thick coating of dust, and the absence of artificial lighting, there was nothing to distinguish this living room from what it must have been like before the EMP had happened.

"Is she going to be OK?" said Dan.

Rob shrugged. "Who knows. I'm no doctor, but I think so."

Dan frowned with worry. He didn't know the woman, but she'd saved his life. He felt indebted to her.

Rob seemed to sense that Dan was worried, and he added, "Don't worry, kid. She's going to be fine. I've seen worse wounds plenty of times. And we should be fine here for a little while. Trust me, these scroungers go for the easiest house, even if that means the most danger. If there's an open door, that'll be like a magnet for them. And they haven't hit this area really hard yet, judging by how this house is totally undisturbed."

Dan didn't quite believe Rob. After all, a man had just broken into the house next door. Surely they didn't really have that much time here.

Seemingly out of nowhere, Dan was feeling a deep well of emotion shifting in him. He didn't know quite what it was.

He was trying not to let the tears form in his eyes. He couldn't remember the last time that he'd cried. Maybe back when he was a little kid and he'd been told that his parents weren't coming to see him. Actually, he didn't remember the specifics of it at all. That was how long ago it was. It was just a memory.

He hadn't cried when his grandmother had died. Or his grandfather.

But all that emotion was still there. And now, everything seemed so hopeless.

It was easy, when things were happening, when there was something to do, to keep all that emotion at bay, to keep it buried deep somewhere.

But here he was in a living room as if the EMP had never happened. In this brief moment of rest, everything came flooding back.

"We've got to come up with a plan," said Dan, speaking more to distract himself than out of real necessity.

"You're right," said Rob. "But I've been thinking that way since the EMP, and every time I come up with a plan, something comes along and knocks me on my ass."

Dan had been noticing that the way Rob had been speaking had been changing. At first, he'd sounded like some posh gentleman. Now, he was speaking more like the people Dan had grown up with and worked with at the hardware store.

"What'd you do before the EMP?" said Dan. He asked out of curiosity in an attempt to further distract himself, and also with a sense of practicality. If Rob had some special skills from a previous profession, maybe he could help them somehow.

"Oh," said Rob, casually. "I did a lot of things."

"Like what?"

Rob leaned back further in the rocking chair. "I was a valet parker for a few years after high school. That was OK until I got bored with it. So I passed a couple tests, got a scholarship, and went to school. Next thing I knew, I was a lawyer at a high-power firm."

"So you must be really smart, then?"

Rob laughed. "I don't know how smart I was. I wasn't taking to the law life that well. I was bored, so I quit. One day, I just walked out of the office. I remember walking down the street, taking off my tie and tossing it into the gutter. One of the firm partners called me and asked where the hell I was. You see, I had clients I was supposed to be meeting with."

"But you just walked off?"

Rob laughed again. "That's right, just walked the hell out of there. I told them I was quitting. They told me I had another five years before I'd get any kind of pension at all. I told them they could keep it. I walked right down the street to the bar, went on a bender for a week."

"A bender?"

"I wasn't a drunk, but that week I drank more than I probably have in my whole life."

Dan didn't know what to say. He'd never even touched alcohol. "How'd you get out of that?"

"Next thing I knew, the buzz wore off and I was working as a garbage man in the city. So I said what the hell and I worked there for another five years."

"Then what happened?"

"The EMP happened, that's what. I liked working sanitation. It was a hell of a lot better than being a lawyer, as far as I was concerned. Out in the fresh air. Well, it wasn't always so fresh, but you get used to the smell after a while. I got to enjoy the sunshine, the rain, just about everything. Beats working in an office."

"I don't think you'll ever be stuck in an office again," said Dan.

Rob laughed. "I thought you didn't have a sense of humor, kid," he said. "But you're surprising me at every turn. Come on, let's see what this house has to offer. Maybe we can scrounge up some food."

Rob checked the pulse of the woman before they left the room, saying that she looked like she was doing fine and that the wound hadn't started bleeding again.

Not much light entered the rest of the house, since all the blinds were drawn, and Rob said it'd be best to keep them that way. But gradually their eyes got accustomed to the lower levels of light.

Most of the house looked like it had been completely untouched. There were only a couple isolated spots where some evidence of commotion could be seen. One of the upstairs bedrooms had clothes spread out all over the floor.

"Looks like they were in a hurry to leave their house," said Rob, gently kicking at the clothing with his boot.

Many of the dresser drawers were opened. One of the had even been removed completely from the dresser and it now lay on the floor.

"What do you think happened to the people who lived here?" said Dan. "Where'd they all go?"

"Everyone was worried that someone was invading," said Rob. "That was the word on the street around here when the EMP first hit. If their car happened to still work, then they left in that. If it didn't, they got a ride with whoever'd take them. Or they left by foot. People were desperate."

"Why didn't you leave?"

"It's a long story," said Rob, a look of sadness crossing his face. "Let's not go into that now."

Dan didn't want to intrude too much. He figured it was something personal. Maybe Rob had lost someone important to him. He hadn't asked about Rob's family, and Rob hadn't mentioned anyone.

"Why are some of the cars working and some aren't?" said Dan. "I thought they'd all be knocked out of commission."

"So you know how an EMP works?" said Rob, an eyebrow rising in surprise.

"Doesn't everyone, at this point?"

"I've met a lot who haven't."

"I heard about it at the hardware store where I used to work," said Dan. "One of the guys there was always talking about it. Most people didn't pay any attention to him. They said he was paranoid and all that. But I'd listen to his stories sometimes."

Rob nodded. "So I don't know either why some vehicles are affected and others aren't." He shrugged his shoulders. "Frankly, it's been the least of my worries. But now that you ask, I guess everyone has their own idea about how something like an EMP is supposed to work, and then reality turns out to be much different."

"Makes sense," said Dan. "Hey, check this out."

They'd just entered the kitchen, which stank of rotting trash, and Dan had started opening cupboards at random. Some of them were just filled with dishes, as well as pots and pans. Normal kitchen stuff for the most part. But one of them was full of packaged food.

There were boxes of crackers, boxes of pasta, cans of tuna fish, smoked oysters. All sorts of non-perishable foods.

Rob started clicking his tongue. "Looks like we're in luck," he said, grabbing as much of it as he could in his arms. "See if there's any silverware in one of the drawers."

Sure enough, Dan found forks, knives, and spoons

neatly arranged in one of the drawers, just as they would have been in his own house.

"Let's have ourselves a little feast," said Rob, settling down in one of the kitchen chairs, dumping the food onto the table, and immediately going for the oysters. He pulled the tab back on the top of the tin, greedily grabbed a fork from Dan, and speared one of the smoked oysters on his fork. He held it there in front of his face for a long moment, apparently savoring the idea of eating it before actually put it in his mouth. "I've always loved oysters," he said, before devouring the oyster in a single bite. "Wish we had some hot sauce."

"This is great we've got some food," said Dan, still standing. He was starting to feel nervous again, about the possibility of someone getting into the house.

"Come on, kid, sit down and eat something. You'll feel better."

"Yeah," said Dan. "I will. But shouldn't we be on the lookout for more of the scrounger people?"

Rob nodded with his mouth full. "Yeah," he said, once he'd finished chewing. He'd already eaten almost the entire tin of oysters, and was now preparing to drink down the oil that they'd been soaking in. "We should. But like I said, we can't leave with her in that condition. So there's nothing to do for now but wait. And while we wait, we might as well eat."

"What are we going to do if they try to break in here? They were just trying to break in next door, after all."

"We'll fight when the time comes, if it comes," said Rob, who'd moved onto a package of salted crackers. "Here, you'd better eat something. Don't worry, we'll save something for her too, for when she wakes up."

Dan was a little thrown off by Rob's cavalier attitude,

but he realized that there really wasn't any way they could mount a proper watch on the house. Putting one of them outside was too risky. And if one of them was upstairs, looking out one of the windows, it'd be obvious from whoever was approaching on the street.

What was more, there were only two of them. And there were four directions they could be approached from.

Maybe Rob was right. The best notice they could get that someone had arrived was sound, the sound of someone breaking a window or trying to break a door. Rob had locked the door behind them, so unless the next scrounger had a lock pick kit and some skill, they'd hear whoever it was.

Dan sat down opposite Rob, and Rob passed him the crackers. Dan ate them with relish, shoving many of them in his mouth at once.

"I didn't realize how hungry I was," said Dan, speaking with his mouth full of food.

"That's the way it goes," said Rob. "It's the adrenaline. It rises when we're hungry, and it keeps our hunger away. But it does it by breaking down muscle tissue to turn into glucose. It's called gluconeogenesis."

Dan nodded, but he wasn't really listening that carefully, and he wasn't sure he'd understand if he had been. The important thing now was food. Eating it. Not understanding how near-starvation worked.

Dan quickly moved on from crackers to a tin of tuna, which had a quick-open top to it. The first bite in his mouth, it seemed as if nothing had ever tasted so good. And Dan didn't even like tuna. In fact, he'd never liked seafood of any kind before. Until now, that was.

"You think we should go check on her?" said Dan,

reaching for a jar of unopened peanut butter. He'd never thought that he'd be so interested in eating peanut butter. He'd always hated it. Up until now, that is, when it meant plenty of concentrated calories.

Rob shook his head. "In a minute," he said. "She'll be fine. Don't worry."

"You've done a surgery like that before, then?"

"A couple of them," said Rob, vaguely. "Some of them worked out, some didn't."

With his stomach starting to get full, Dan felt like he had enough courage to ask Rob what had happened to him right after the EMP.

"How did you survive this long?" said Dan, speaking more abruptly than he would have liked.

Rob eyed him for a moment without saying anything. For a second, Dan was worried he'd caused a tense moment. After all, he'd just met Rob, even though it felt, in some ways, that they'd known each other much longer. Probably because of what they'd been through already.

Rob shrugged. "I just kept on going," he said. "That's about the best anyone can do." He opened up a package of cookies, and started flipping through them with his fingers, apparently trying to find and select the biggest cookie of them all. "So what's your plan, kid? Is there any point in asking where you're headed, if you've got any plans? Or are you simply on the run, living from day to day like the rest of us?"

Dan found himself talking more than he had in a long time. Maybe it was the food, or maybe it was just having company. His grandfather had been sick at the end, uttering only a few words here and there. Dan had spent most of his time since the EMP in worried, panicked silence.

Dan told Rob about his grandfather, about the trucks he'd seen. He told him about waiting and waiting, not knowing what was going on. He told him about the voice on the radio that he'd gotten working, a man named Max, who had a camp setup. He told him about the soldiers, about his friend from the hardware store who'd died. He told him about the man that he'd killed, and he told him about how the injured woman had saved his life, and then how Rob had saved it again.

"So this Max, what happened with him?"

"I don't know," said Dan. "I didn't get a chance to talk to him again. But I know where his camp is."

"So that's where you're headed?"

"If I can get there, yeah," said Dan. "But I don't know if I can really make it. I lost my pack. I lost the gear I had. I'd barely gotten far from my house when those soldiers picked me up. I wasn't strong enough. I didn't have a gun... I did what I could. I don't know if I'll ever make it all the way north to where Max is."

"What kind of setup does this Max have?" said Rob.

"Oh, I don't know exactly. It doesn't sound like anything really advanced or anything."

"So what's the reason to head there?"

"Well, he's out in the woods, away from all the chaos. About as much as you can be, I suppose. And there are deer there, plenty of them."

"So they've got food, then?"

"Sounds like it. Not like this, of course," said Dan, gesturing to the spread of packaged food laid out on the table between them.

"More nutritious, though," said Rob. "All natural. That's the real way to eat."

Dan nodded, not really knowing what Rob was talking about.

"And how many of them are out there at this camp of Max's?"

"Uh, I'm not sure. Half a dozen or so? Max kept it all pretty close to his chest with that kind of stuff." Keeping something close to your chest was an expression Dan had heard his grandfather use from time to time.

"Sounds like a smart guy," said Rob, who then fell silent, except for chewing some crackers, and cracking open another tin of smoked oysters.

"You seem like you're lost in thought," said Dan, after a few minutes.

"Maybe I am, kid," said Rob. "You want to know what I was thinking?"

"What?"

"I was wondering if Max would have room for three more at this camp of his, if it still exists, that is."

"You mean you'd come with me?"

"Why not? I don't have long left living the way I'm living now. With every house I break into, I know it could be my last. I've had too many close calls already. I'd thought about getting out, into the woods somewhere, but it seemed too hard to do on my own. But a small community, banding together, that's the real way to do it."

Dan found himself smiling widely. For the first time in days, he felt like he had some hope.

If Rob was coming along, he was sure they'd be able to get to the camp. No matter what it took. Rob was big and strong. He had a gun. Dan was just a small little lost kid.

"What did you mean about if it's still there?" said Dan, suddenly wondering what Rob had meant.

"Well, let's just not get our hopes up too much. If

there's one thing I've learned about life since the EMP, it's that nothing's permanent."

Dan felt his stomach sinking a little, but he shoved a couple more salted crackers into his mouth to make up for it.

12

GEORGIA

Georgia hadn't seen any deer that morning. Maybe she'd gone out too late. She didn't have a watch, and she had to guess the time based on the sun. It wasn't hard to do, but it was difficult to be more exact than within a couple hours.

She was trudging on back to the camp. She'd ended up walking deeper into the woods than she'd initially intended. But when she hadn't seen any signs of deer, she'd decided, almost unconsciously, to press on and on.

Georgia was out of breath. Her back was hurting her, throbbing with pain. She'd never had a lick of back pain before getting shot. She didn't know if it was from the actual injury or the impromptu surgery that'd been done in the back of a moving vehicle.

She hadn't mentioned the back pain to anyone. For one thing, she couldn't complain about a surgery that had saved her life. But the main thing was that Georgia didn't want anyone to know that she was still in pain, that she wasn't as strong as she was pretending to be.

Sure, she was better than she had been. By a long shot.

But aside from the back pain, the place where she'd been shot still occasionally throbbed with pain. She hadn't figured out if there were certain ways of moving her body that made it worse or better.

So she'd decided to try to ignore it. Pretend it wasn't there.

She knew that Max's leg still gave him problems, and she never saw him talk about that.

But it was something deeper, something deep inside Georgia. Ever since she'd been a kid, she'd been independent. She'd always been strong. When she'd become a mother, she'd only gotten stronger. She'd had to be for her kids. There hadn't been any other way.

Georgia could deal with the pain fairly well, but it hard to fight against the weakness that seemed to consume her whole body. The weakness wasn't as overwhelming as it had been weeks earlier. She was stronger now, but maybe she'd pushed herself too far.

As she walked back to camp, she found her feet almost dragging on the ground. She found herself walking slower and slower.

OK. She had to take a break. No one was around to see her do it.

She sat down, leaning her back against a thick tree trunk.

She kept her rifle out and ready, laying it sideways across her stretched-out legs.

Since she hadn't sat in proper furniture for weeks and weeks now, a tree felt almost like a luxury whereas before the EMP, she would have mentally complained about the hardness, the ridges in the bark. She would have felt how uncomfortable it all was. Of course, she would have never voiced any of this. But it was still there, inside her.

The forest was quiet and calm. Georgia took a deep breath of the fresh air.

She'd rarely noticed just how polluted the air had been back in the suburbs. People talked about city pollution, but it was everywhere too. It was just that people didn't normally have anything to compare it to.

Before the EMP, sometimes, coming back from a hunting trip, Georgia could tell the difference. But it didn't last long, the memory of the fresh forest air faded quickly as normal life and its obligations quickly took over. Sadie and James had needed to get to school. Georgia'd needed to get to her various jobs, clean the house, cook for the kids. She'd rarely had any time for herself, except on those hunting trips.

Georgia wondered how the air was now back in the suburbs, and even the cities. Would the thin, almost imperceptible, smog just slowly fade away? There couldn't be many cars and trucks still operating. And slowly all the remaining engines would either grind down into disrepair, or remain rusting somewhere as gas become impossible to obtain.

The woods were calm and peaceful. Georgia breathed a sigh of relief. The pain was better now that she was sitting.

It wasn't too cold. Just a bit of a chill to the air.

Soon enough it'd be spring, and the trees would be green once again. There'd be wild flowers blossoming and the air would have that sweet freshness.

Life had been hard since the EMP. Nearly impossible. There'd been so many moments where it had seemed like it was finally the end that Georgia had completely lost count of them.

But maybe things would settle down. The country, and

maybe the whole world, was going through a difficult change, a complete upheaval of the established order. After that, when the dust settled, maybe they'd be left with a calm, peaceful life.

If it hadn't been for the violence, the struggle to survive, Georgia probably would have preferred the simple, natural life, compared to life in the suburbs. She'd only been there because of the kids. They'd needed a good education.

Georgia took another deep breath of the fresh, cool air, savoring the taste and feeling of it as she held it in her lungs.

Maybe things would work out OK. Maybe they'd make it. Maybe life would be better, more enjoyable, less full of the bullshit that Georgia had hated about modern life.

A woman like her could really thrive in this new environment.

All they had to do was get through the tough parts, the changes, where violence was the rule of law and life was cheap to the point of being worthless.

She was realistic. She knew she couldn't let her thoughts get ahead of herself.

There was still plenty of work to be done. At the moment, her work was shooting deer.

Maybe she'd get lucky and stumble across some on the way back to camp, even though it was a little late for them.

Georgia stood up slowly, holding onto the tree trunk for support.

Before she could take her first step, she heard a twig snap off in the distance, somewhere in front of her, to the south.

If she was lucky, it'd be a deer.

If she was unlucky, it'd be someone. Maybe the people who'd stolen their food when the mob had come.

It'd be just like them, cowards that they apparently were, to approach her when she was alone.

Had they followed her?

She didn't think so. She'd been too careful. She'd moved quietly. She'd checked her surroundings constantly, always making sure to look behind her.

Georgia didn't move except to get her rifle ready. She slid her finger over the trigger, where it rested, waiting.

Georgia didn't put her eye to the scope. Not yet. The sound hadn't sounded *that* far off, and she didn't want to let tunnel vision allow her to miss something important off her periphery.

The pain in her back was still there, as was the weakness. She tried to keep her thoughts focused on the present, but they kept seeming to slip, her mind winding its way back to her children at camp. Would they be safe without her? John and Cynthia were capable. But they weren't her, and Max was off somewhere, his return uncertain.

Another sound. This one slighter, quieter than the last.

Something poked its way out from behind a tree.

It was a deer head.

Georgia breathed a sigh of relief.

Not only was it not a dangerous person, but it was food.

Georgia put her eye to the scope, and, without moving, got the deer right in her crosshairs.

Most hunters went for the heart or the lungs first. It was easier than a bullet to the brain.

But a bullet to the brain would drop the deer in one

shot. And Georgia knew she could pull it off. She just had to wait until the deer emerged a little farther. She wanted a clean shot.

The deer moved, inching forward, its head bent down as it searched for food on the ground.

But before Georgia could pull the trigger, a shot rang out.

Georgia threw herself to the ground. She was on her stomach, her rifle in front of her, her finger still on the trigger.

The deer jumped forward, looking startled.

It was running at top speed. Right towards Georgia, who it didn't seem to see.

Blood trailed behind the deer, spurting out of its body.

Someone had been hunting that same deer, and they weren't as good a shot as Georgia. They'd hit the deer, but it hadn't been a killing shot.

Another shot rang out.

This time the deer fell. It lay there, about twenty feet in front of Georgia. Its eyes were wide open and seemed to stare at her.

Georgia's heart was pounding.

What should she do? Run? Stand her ground?

She didn't know how effective running would be given her fatigue, her weakness. But maybe the adrenaline would help her. She was sure she could do it.

But while she'd been deciding, a figure had emerged from off in the distance.

A man. Tall. Big beard. Long hair. Wearing camouflage that didn't do much to disguise his body in the current climate.

He carried a rifle at his side in one hand.

He was casting looks around, trying to spot the deer he'd shot.

In a moment, his eyes would land on Georgia. And it was too late to run.

She wasn't going to shoot him. Not now. Not yet. It wasn't right. For all she knew, he could be just like her, a good person just trying to survive. He could even have been someone that she'd met once on a hunting trip, someone she'd sat around the fire later with and shared a beer with.

The man was getting closer. Georgia could see his face clearly now, but he still hadn't seen her or the deer. He had a wide face, a deep brow, and an intense way of squinting at his surroundings. Maybe he'd lost his glasses and didn't have great vision.

But she couldn't count on it.

Georgia would make the first move.

"Hands in the air," shouted Georgia.

The man froze.

But he didn't drop his gun.

His eyes moved over to her.

"Drop the gun," shouted Georgia.

"Or what? What's a little lost lady like you going to do to me?"

"You already know the answer. Drop it. You have three seconds."

The man took a single long step closer to Georgia. The distance wasn't much now. But still enough.

Georgia trigger finger quavered.

She was counting in her head. Three... two...

If she counted it out, she wasn't a murderer. She'd given the guy options. If he didn't want to play by her rules, then that was on him. Not her.

She wasn't going to give second chances. She'd fire.

She may have been ethical, but she wasn't weak.

"Fine!"

The man suddenly dropped his rifle onto the ground and raised his hands high over his head.

Georgia eased up the tension on her finger.

"Stay where you are!"

"I don't mean any harm," said the man. "I'm just trying to get dinner. And I don't react well to being told what to do by strangers with guns. Never have."

Georgia could relate. In a sense.

"Who are you?"

"Does it matter anymore? I'll give you my name, but it doesn't mean much."

"Just do it."

"William Baxter, but people call me Will."

"And what are you doing here?"

"What am I doing here?" He laughed. "What everyone's doing, I guess. Trying to survive."

"Are you with anyone else?"

"Just me."

"You know anything about a camp near here?"

"A camp? Just my own."

"Where's your camp?"

"Over by the big gully, over on the eastern end."

Georgia hadn't been there. She didn't even know if there was a gully.

And for all Georgia knew, everything coming out of this man's mouth could be a lie.

If he was one of the ones who'd stolen their food, what incentive would he have to admit it? Absolutely none.

She could take his rifle and leave him there. But that might as well be a death sentence for the man. Without his rifle, he wouldn't be able to hunt. Or to defend himself.

It was always the same problem. Trying to tell if someone was out to hurt them or not.

That was the problem with being ethical, without shooting to kill and not bothering with questions. It was the problem she and Max and everyone else had grown tired of facing.

But not tired to the point of changing their ways.

Not yet, at least.

Georgia stood up slowly. She was going to let him go. It wasn't an easy choice. But it was the right thing to do.

Suddenly, bark from the tree behind Georgia exploded. The pieces hit her in the back, pelting against her jacket.

The gunshot rang out.

It must have been far away.

They'd missed.

Georgia threw herself on the ground again.

The man, William Baxter, if that was really his name, was reaching for his rifle on the ground.

Georgia didn't look through the scope, but she knew she had him. She pulled the trigger.

The shot rang out. The gun kicked.

But Baxter didn't fall.

Somehow, she'd missed.

Baxter was closing the distance between them fast. She saw his face clearly, the anger contorting it. His eyes burned with intensity.

He was holding his rifle in one hand high above his head, apparently intending to use it like a club.

Georgia had mere seconds to get off another shot. She was keeping calm as he closed the distance, waiting for the moment that she could be sure her shot would be the final one.

But before she could fire, the sniper off in the distance fired again. They missed, but the bullet lodged itself into the ground in front of Georgia's face, sending dirt into her eyes.

She heard the shot ringing out after she was momentarily blinded.

Baxter was still coming at her. Georgia could hear him, hear his feet pounding on the ground.

She couldn't see much. Debris had gotten into both her eyes, which were filling up with tears as her eyes tried to clear themselves.

Georgia didn't have much of a chance of hitting him. But she pulled the trigger anyway.

The gun kicked and the shot rang out.

Despite the ringing in her ears, she could still hear Baxter.

It was too late. She'd missed.

Georgia was blinking rapidly, trying to get her eyes working again.

She felt the rifle hit her in the shoulder. Baxter had swung it down like a club. It made a harsh sound as it slammed into her. Her old injury flared up. Pain ran through her.

Baxter was suddenly on top of her, pressing his knees into her back. He was heavy, and she was pressed into the dirt.

Her rifle was knocked out of her hands.

Baxter growled something, but she didn't hear what it was. It sounded more like the sound an animal would make rather than English.

Georgia wasn't going to give up.

Baxter's hands were around her throat from behind. He was trying to strangle her. As quickly as possible.

His hands were strong and rough. He had a firm grip around her neck and he squeezed. Hard.

Georgia felt the loss of oxygen.

But she wasn't going down without a fight.

Her eyes were finally clear of the debris. Tears flowed down her cheeks and her eyes still burned, but she could see.

She had a handgun with her. But she didn't have much of a chance of shooting him in the position he was in.

She had a knife, too, but if she could get to it, she'd be stabbing wildly behind her in the hopes of catching him.

She didn't have much time left before she was unconscious. Mere seconds.

Her rifle wasn't far from her, lying there in the dirt.

Georgia reached out suddenly and swiftly, so that he'd have no time to stop her.

She seized the rifle around the muzzle with one hand. She brought it up swiftly, raising her arm off the ground as fast and hard as she could. The rifle followed, swinging through the air.

The rifle collided with Baxter. Georgia didn't know where, but she heard it. He grunted in pain as hit him.

The rifle fell away from her hand. She couldn't hold onto it. She was getting too weak.

The hands around her neck suddenly relaxed.

Georgia's instinct was to gasp for breath, to lie there and recover. But there wasn't time for that.

Still sputtering for air, Georgia made one final attempt to get out from under him. She twisted around, moving her body as fast as she could.

Now she was face up, and she brought her fist up. She punched him right in the face.

He grunted in pain again. He was bleeding from his head where the rifle must have struck him.

Georgia felt weak and energized at the same time. Her injuries sapped the strength from her, and now she was dealing with strangulation. At the same time, the adrenaline coursed through her. And even more powerful than the adrenaline was the knowledge that she had to get back to James and Sadie.

She had to. There was no other option.

She had to keep low to the ground. The sniper was still out there. Although he didn't seem to be a good enough shot to distinguish between Baxter, who was presumably his friend, and Georgia.

But Georgia didn't want to risk it.

Georgia was on all fours, in a semi-crouch position.

Baxter was still reeling in pain, but he'd fixed his eyes once again on Georgia. There was only one thing in those eyes, and that was his intention to kill.

The rifle lay on the ground between them. They weren't far apart.

Georgia was already reaching for her handgun in its holster.

She had her hand around the handle.

She was drawing it. Her hand and arm felt weak, but she had to keep going.

Baxter had gone for the rifle. It was in his hand now.

Georgia had the handgun out. She raised her arm, holding it straight out.

Baxter was raising the rifle.

Georgia took aim.

She pulled the trigger.

The gun kicked and Georgia's ears rang.

It seemed as if the bullet had hit Baxter right in the heart. A good, clean shot.

Baxter fell forward, facedown onto the earth. Georgia glimpsed the look of surprise and anger as he fell.

There wasn't any time to savor the victory, to savor the feeling of being alive.

The sniper was still out there. And maybe there was more than one.

Georgia was still gasping for air. Her brain didn't seem to be working quite right. Her neck burned with pain where his fingers had been.

Georgia had to get down as low as she could again. Shelter would be good. But she'd have to crawl behind a tree. She knew the rough direction of the sniper, but not the location.

Georgia fell to the ground more than she got there herself.

She lay there, trying to catch her breath, trying to breathe.

Someone was out there. And they wanted her dead.

13

Max and Mandy remained crouched behind stacks of cardboard boxes. They were trying not to move much or make any sounds at all.

They couldn't see what was happening without peeking out, and they didn't want to do that.

Light flooded the whole area. One of the cargo doors was open, but Max hadn't yet heard any sounds. No greetings. No shouts or commands. Nothing.

They waited.

All Max could hear were footsteps.

Now there was some grunting. Some indecipherable sounds. Maybe something being set down? It was a cargo area, after all. Maybe a delivery was being made.

But a delivery? It didn't make sense.

"What should we do?" whispered Mandy, speaking directly into Max's ear in an incredibly soft voice.

With the other noises, there wasn't much chance a whisper like that could be heard.

Max could feel Mandy's hot breath in his ear. He tried not to let it distract him.

Max shook his head at her, indicating that he didn't know.

Mandy put her mouth back against his ear. "Do you think it has anything to do with the drugs?"

"The drugs?" whispered Max, using the same technique.

"Didn't you see the drugs lying around? All those people are high on something. There were needles and everything."

Max shook his head to let her know he hadn't seen it.

How had he missed it? That wasn't like him. Then again, there hadn't been much time.

So that added a new piece to the puzzle.

Before Max could think about it any further, someone finally spoke.

"OK, boss, I've got it all distributed."

"You got everyone a good supply?"

Max couldn't hear the next thing. Just some inaudible mumbling.

"OK, then. Who's it going to be?"

"What about that one?"

"Too thin."

"He's only going to get thinner."

Max was listening as carefully as he could, trying to pick up not just the tone of the conversation and the meaning, but trying to see if he could glean some information about who these men were.

If they needed to fight their way out, knowing something about them ahead of time would be helpful.

A quick glance exchanged with Mandy assured Max that she didn't know what the conversation was about either.

"All right, you're right. Load him up."

Were they taking one of the workers away?

Would there be some kind of protest, a fight? After all, it didn't sound like it was a volunteer program they were running.

But there was nothing. No fight. No struggle. Hardly even a word. Just some more mumbling, and a couple words here and there from the two men.

The next thing Max knew, the metal door was shutting again. It slammed down into the concrete and once again the room was dark.

It'd take Max's eyes a little while to adjust. He'd have to wait until then before he made any moves.

For now, it seemed like they were in the clear.

As Max waited for his eyes to adjust, he felt his pulse with his fingers. His heart rate was going down, but it was still elevated. His body had been ready for a fight that hadn't happened.

"What the hell just happened?" whispered Mandy through the darkness.

"No idea," said Max. "We'll wait a couple more minutes and then we'll find out."

"You're worried they'll come back?"

"It's a possibility."

So they waited.

Maybe they should just leave, get out of the whole rest stop as soon as possible. This wasn't any of their business, whatever it was that was going on.

But they couldn't leave just yet. Whoever had come and opened the cargo door might still be out there, waiting. They'd see Max and Mandy as they left the building.

After enough time had passed, it didn't seem like the cargo door would open again.

"Come on," whispered Max. "Let's see what happened. Then we'll get out of here."

Slowly, Max and Mandy left their hiding place and began walking through the candle-lit area.

People were laying on the wooden pallets just before. Some were curled up. Many lay on their backs, spread-eagle, with their mouths open and their eyes glazed over.

There was a young man with long hair on one of the pallets who looked dazed. Next to him, there was a small bag of white powder lying on the ground. A needle and syringe lay next to it.

"So this is what they were giving them, you think?" said Mandy, bending down to examine the baggie more closely. "What do you think it is?"

"Careful," said Max. "Don't touch it."

"Why not?" said Mandy, her hand mere inches away from the bag.

"Before the EMP, I read news stories of heroin laced with a drug called Fentanyl. It's a synthetic opiate that's many times more potent than anything else, active in the micrograph range and very deadly. Even just touching it can lead to fatalities."

"Oh," said Mandy in surprise, pulling her hand away. "But it wouldn't kill me, would it?" She looked worried, and wiped her hand on her pant leg. "I mean, if he injected it..."

"Probably has a high tolerance," said Max, peering at the man. "Whatever that stuff is, it sure seems like the men who were here were dropping off drugs. Everyone's more out of it than before they arrived."

"They really are," said Mandy, casting her eyes around the room at the other half-awake figures. "But why would someone come here and give drugs to a bunch of these employees? It's really weird."

Max nodded. "It's weird, yeah," he said, his eyes falling on Jones, who was off in a new corner, curled up in the fetal position. "Let's see if our friend Jones has anything to say about it."

They walked over, and Max nudged Jones with the toe of his boot. "What's this all about, Jones? Who were those people?"

"They're helping us," muttered Jones, his voice slurred.

"Helping you how? By bringing you drugs?"

Jones nodded sleepily.

"That's not going to help you," said Mandy, sounding angry.

"Why are they doing this?" said Max.

Jones didn't answer.

"What are they getting out of it? Are they taking something from you? What are you giving them?"

Jones looked up at Max with half-opened eyes. "They take us sometimes."

"They take you sometimes?" said Mandy. "What the hell are you talking about? He's just talking gibberish. Come on, Max. Let's get out of here."

"No," said Max. "I think he's trying to say something. You're saying they're taking some of you away?"

Jones nodded.

"Like one at a time? They take one of you each time they come?"

Jones nodded and then he closed his eyes, going back into his sleepy trance state.

"What the hell?" muttered Mandy. "They're keeping them all here, and taking them away one by one? What in the world would be the goal in something like that? Whatever it is, it's sick."

"Yeah," said Max. "I can't figure it out either." His eyes kept moving around the room, studying it. "What it means to me is that people are starting to get organized."

"Organized?"

"Yeah. There's some group out there that has the basics of survival already covered. They've got resources and the time to come here and do whatever it is they're doing. They've got access to not only food but drugs, and they have some strange and probably twisted goal in mind. Groups like the militia in the suburbs, and the compound, they're all going to start growing in power. Some will take over others, consuming them and growing bigger and more powerful."

"Doesn't sound good."

"No," said Max. "No, it doesn't."

"I wish we could have gotten farther away from the East Coast," said Mandy. "I wish we could have made it far out to some rural area in the middle of the country, like your original plan."

"Well," said Max. "We might end up doing that someday. But for now, it seems like our camp is our best option. We can hide out there while whatever it is here goes on."

"We just have to get back there."

Max nodded. "Do you think we should try to help them? These people here?"

Max didn't say anything for a moment. "They're too far gone," he said. "And it's not like they didn't have a choice."

Mandy nodded stiffly. "Well then, let's get out of here. I don't like the idea of being stuck in here again if those people come back."

"We'll go out the way we came in," said Max.

14

S omehow Janet had gotten away from the house. Somehow she hadn't run into any more of the militia members. Somehow, she was still alive.

It didn't make sense. She should be dead. She knew it intellectually, and she knew it in her body, deep in her bones that felt cold.

Her muscles ached and her head pounded with the worst headache she'd ever had. Her skin was covered in a cold sweat and her heart pounded in staccato intervals.

She should have lost hope, hope of killing Sarge. She should have taken this as an opportunity to just get away. She could start over somewhere new. She could get out into the woods and live by herself. She could hunt and gather, like her ancient ancestors.

No one got away from the militia. Not former members, at least. She was beyond lucky, and she should have taken the opportunity and run with it.

But she wasn't going to do that.

She was going to find Sarge if it was the last thing she did.

She was sitting next to a small creek. The water flowed slowly around the rocks and pebbles.

It wasn't yet dark out. She'd spent the day hiding in the reeds at the edge of a park, and when the sun had started to fall in the sky, she'd woken up and crawled to this creek not far away.

It might have been around four o'clock. But it was hard to tell without a watch.

Why hadn't they found her as she slept?

Maybe it was just luck. Maybe she'd gotten far enough out of their way.

Or maybe they'd stopped looking for her. Maybe something else had come up.

A manhunt, after all, took a lot of resources. The militia was large, but not infinite.

She had no food with her. No supplies other than her weapons.

She had her knife, a long fixed-blade, her shotgun, and a handgun.

The shotgun lay beside her. It was fully loaded. Three shells. She picked it up and checked it again, just to make sure.

She had more shells with her. But for the handgun, she had nothing more than what was in it.

Her stomach was empty. But hunger wasn't on her mind. It was just revenge. And nothing more.

She tried to slow her breathing in an attempt to clear her mind. She needed to think clearly if she was going to accomplish what she wanted to.

She needed a plan.

The way she saw it, she had two options. She'd get to Sarge and finish him. Right away.

If she waited around, if she delayed any longer, the

hunger and fatigue would soon overcome her. She'd be too weak to continue fighting. If she took that route, she'd have to hole up somewhere for a few days and get some food, make preparations, make more elaborate plans.

What she wanted to do was simply rush off and fight. Right now. No more waiting. No more hesitating.

But she knew that wouldn't work as well as a real plan. Rushing off now meant rushing off to die.

The fights from yesterday were still fresh in her mind. The dead men's eyes were still fresh in her memory. The sounds they'd made when dying were still fresh in her ears.

Something'd been different about those kills. She wasn't going to overanalyze it.

But she knew that the memories were going to continue to haunt her. They'd distract her. If she found some basement or home to hide out in, some food to eat, she'd have to deal with those thoughts and memories for the next few days.

She'd be all alone. Nothing but her own mind and her painful memories to torment her.

She knew she couldn't deal with it.

She knew that going to find Sarge now would end in quick death. She knew that she'd never get anywhere near Sarge. She knew it was hopeless.

But she was going to do it anyway.

Most likely, she'd be gunned down by the nearest militia soldier on patrol. Most likely, a description of her had been passed around to all members. They'd had plenty of time to do it.

It was the easiest way out. A sort of suicide. An end to everything. Going out in a blaze, not of glory but of something else entirely, would be the easier approach.

And she wanted easy. Everything had been too hard. Far too hard.

Janet stood up. Her boots sunk a little into the wet dirt by the creek. She walked over to the creek, bent down, and splashed some of the cool, almost icy, water onto her face. She took more of it in her cupped hands and dumped it on her hair, over her head. She stood there with water running down around her ears, over her nose. She stuck out her tongue and tasted some of it.

Janet had no compass or maps. But she didn't need any. She knew this area as well as any of the other militia members.

Taking in a deep breath, she walked straight across the little creek. It didn't matter if her boots got a little wet.

She crossed through the reeds on the edge of the park and started walking straight across the field.

There was a baseball field. The grass was overgrown.

She was out in the open. She wasn't trying to hide herself. She wasn't trying to sneak around.

It'd be easier this way.

It didn't take long for her to be spotted. After all, there were patrols everywhere.

On the road that ran parallel to the far side of the park, an old Jeep rumbled along slowly.

Janet glanced at it and kept walking.

She had her shotgun in both hands. Her grip was tight. Her finger was on the trigger.

She kept walking, knowing that they'd seen her. There was no way they couldn't have. She was a solitary figure walking alone with a gun. No one else dared to go outside in this area. No one but the militia.

She heard the Jeep's engine. Louder now. Getting closer.

Her eyes darted off to the side. She didn't turn her head.

The Jeep took a sharp turn, heading right towards the curb. It jumped the curb, bouncing violently.

The engine was louder. The Jeep was coming at her, driving across the field.

She kept walking, picking up her pace. It wasn't like there was anywhere to hide. Nothing to duck behind. Nowhere to take shelter.

She didn't bother thinking about how she'd thought she'd have gotten further. She'd thought she'd have gotten a little closer to Sarge. Not all the way there, obviously. But she'd never have suspected they'd have spotted her so quickly.

What she thought about instead was her chances.

She'd taken many of them out already.

What were two more?

She could do it.

But she couldn't ignore the issue any longer. Even if she broke into an all-out sprint, there was no chance she could get off the field and to some kind of shelter before the Jeep reached her.

She stopped and turned towards the Jeep.

It was headed right at her.

She could see two men in it. She could see their faces. They wore the blank expressions so common to those in the militia. They'd disassociated themselves from everything they'd felt.

How else could they survive doing what they were doing, experiencing what they were experiencing?

She didn't have much time. The Jeep was going fast. Maybe forty or fifty miles per hour.

She didn't have many options. If she let it get too close,

it'd be too late to jump to the side. She'd think she could make it, and then it would crash right into her, mowing her down.

Janet leveled the shotgun, pumped it, took aim, and pulled the trigger.

Her aim was good. The gun kicked. Her ears rang. The windshield shattered.

Aiming for a tire would have been useless. They would have just kept driving. It would have hardly slowed them down. It wasn't like in the movies, where shooting out a tire would make the Jeep suddenly flip over and explode. At least, not usually.

The Jeep was still racing towards her.

She dove to the side at the last moment. Hopefully the limited visibility of the driver would be to her advantage.

Sure enough, the Jeep didn't swerve to hit her.

She'd hit the ground hard. The shotgun had somehow fallen from her hands. She reached for it, took it in her hands, and pumped it. The empty shell popped out, landing on the overgrown grass.

The Jeep slammed to a stop not far from her.

Both doors opened.

This was it.

She was on her back, aiming up with the shotgun.

A man she didn't recognize was coming at her, an AR-15 in his hands. His partner, the driver, was still on the other side of the stopped Jeep.

As he raised his weapon, Janet squeezed the trigger. The kick from the shotgun was harsh, her shoulder slamming back into the ground.

The AR-15 clattered to the ground. The soldier fell. Her shot might have caught him in the chest. She didn't know. There wasn't time to look.

Before she could pump the shotgun, a bullet slammed into her left shoulder. The feeling surprised her more than scared her. It felt more like a brick slamming into her than a small projectile piercing her flesh.

She tried to move her arm, but it wouldn't work properly. Her left hand felt weak.

The shotgun slipped out of her left hand. She couldn't maintain her grip.

She tried lifting the shotgun with her right hand, but the gun was long and heavy and her strength suddenly seemed to be sapped. The barrel of the gun hung loosely as she struggled to raise it, pointing into the ground. Useless.

A tall man strode towards her across the grass. He glanced casually at his companion, who lay there moaning.

He held a large caliber pistol. His arm was level and he pointed it at her.

Janet let the shotgun go. It rolled off her and fell onto the grass. She struggled to her feet, reaching for her handgun.

Her left arm hung uselessly at her side. The pain roared through her.

Her right hand found her handgun's handle. But before she could draw it, another shot slammed into her. This time it hit her knee.

Janet collapsed before she registered the pain.

She managed to stick out her arm to keep her head from slamming into the ground.

It was hard not to let go of the handgun. As the pain hit her, all she wanted to do was reach out and grab her knee.

It was the worst pain she'd ever felt. Like the physical

expression of a nightmare, like a monster devouring her from the inside.

The tall soldier continued with long strides to close the gap. He walked at a steady pace. His face was emotionless.

The sun was setting now. Darkness was growing around them.

The baseball field, with its overgrown grass, remained impassive to what was happening. Just a short while ago, it had hosted baseball games and get-togethers. There'd been teenagers there sneaking off to smoke cigarettes and make out. There'd been people who'd stopped there on their lunch breaks and cried into their steering wheels in the parking lot.

All sorts of things had happened there. But nothing like this. A gunfight? Life had been difficult before the EMP. It'd been fraught with problems, personal and otherwise. But the intensity had been dialed up.

Janet managed to get her handgun up. She aimed it, holding her breath and trying not to let the pain distract her.

She pulled the trigger.

The gun kicked.

The shot rang out.

But nothing happened.

She'd missed.

The soldier kept striding towards her. He hadn't reacted to the shot.

Maybe she'd been so far off he hadn't needed to. Or maybe he had a death wish himself and simply didn't care if he got shot.

Janet was getting weaker. Her right arm felt weak now, as if it was filled with lead. She couldn't hold the gun up anymore. Slowly, she felt her arm falling down until it rested on her torso and leg. She couldn't raise it again no matter how much she struggled.

The pain was intense. She closed her eyes for just a moment.

When she opened them again, the tall soldier stood before her. He looked down at her. His eyes had a glazed, distant look to them. His lips, tightly closed, barely moved. There wasn't the twitch of a smile or frown forming at the corner of his lips. There wasn't a look of sadness around his eyes.

There was just nothing.

His gun was pointed right at her head. His arm was stretched out, angling downward towards the ground.

She didn't see him pull the trigger. She didn't even hear the shot.

But she knew that was it.

Finally.

"Come on, kid, don't worry so much about it all. What happens, happens."

"I don't know," said Dan. "I think one of us needs to be awake."

Rob sighed and gently pushed some of the food away from him on the table. "Yeah, you're right," he finally said. "I'll take the first shift."

"It's OK," said Dan. "I'll do it. You get some rest."

"You sure?"

Dan nodded.

"Anyone ever tell you you're mature for your age?"

"Yeah," said Dan. "But that was before the EMP. I bet everyone my age is mature now."

Rob said nothing. "OK," he said. "I'm off to bed. Yell if you need me. Although if something happens, I'm sure I'll hear it."

"Where you going to sleep?"

Rob had initially been saying that they didn't need to keep watch, that they should both just try to get some rest. He'd said they'd hear it if someone broke in.

Dan was still a little worried about Rob's seemingly cavalier approach to safety. Would Rob want to go up to one of the bedrooms so he could rest comfortably? It would mean he'd be farther away if something happened, possibly out of earshot.

"I'll sleep right here in the kitchen. That way I'll be at the back of the house and you'll be at the front of the house."

"You'll be OK on the floor?"

Rob laughed. "I've slept in worse places," he said, getting up from his kitchen table chair and settling down onto the floor. He lay on his back, without even taking off his shoes. His head rested against the hard floor, but it didn't seem to bother him.

So had Dan. But he knew it wasn't easy.

But to Dan's surprise, Rob had already started lightly snoring. He was out like a light.

Dan made his way back into the living room, where the unnamed woman was also asleep.

Dan was tired himself, but he knew that he wouldn't fall asleep. The possibility of one of the scroungers breaking into the house would keep him awake. It was something about his personality. He wasn't the type of person who would let himself succumb to fatigue.

The hours ticked by and Dan found himself lost in thought. His mind drifted here and there, but he managed to keep his thoughts focused on the future, rather than the past. There was no point in dwelling on what had happened, on what he couldn't change.

It seemed like the only course for the future was to get to Max's camp.

But what if that didn't work?

Dan would need to come up with another plan. He

couldn't rely on others.

In his limited experience so far, the populated areas seemed simply too dangerous. It would be a cat and mouse game, hiding in abandoned houses, always waiting for the next intruder, the next soldier or individual who wanted what Dan had.

It'd be a life of constant fights, constant encounters. Dan knew he could live with feeling on edge if that was what it took to survive.

But he knew that he couldn't survive endless encounters. Statistically, there was no reason he should remain alive if he kept fighting. He had no special abilities, no special training or skills that would make him superior.

Either he had to get out into the woods somewhere, away from everything, or he needed a group.

So he'd go to Max's camp. If that didn't work, for whatever reason, he'd press on, finding some safe place. He'd worry about food and drinking water when the time came. Simply not getting shot was the first priority.

The unnamed woman was starting to stir. She opened her eyes and looked around the room.

She saw Dan and made a little jump. Her face showed her fear and surprise. She let out a little yelp.

"It's OK," said Dan, getting up and moving over to her. He spoke in a calm voice, the way one might speak to a spooked horse. "I'm not going to hurt you."

She stared at him with her eyes wide.

"I'm Dan. Remember me? We were captured by the soldiers together."

The woman started to relax a little. Her body started to loosen up, the tenseness slowly fading.

"You got shot," said Dan. "A new friend, a guy named Rob, got the bullet out of you. Do you remember him?"

She nodded.

"Are you still in pain? Can you speak?"

"Yeah," said the woman. Her voice was hoarse.

"What's your name?"

"Olivia," she said.

"Nice to meet you."

She nodded.

"Someone broke into the house when Rob was taking the bullet out of you. We had to fight him off. And now we're in a different house, but in the same area."

"Was he one of the soldiers?"

"No, I don't think so. Just someone looking for food or weapons. Just a regular guy gone mad with desperation. I think the soldiers gave up on us. You're the one who got us out of there, you know? If it wasn't for you, who knows what would have happened to us."

"Don't mention it," said the woman.

Her voice grew less hoarse the more they spoke.

She grew more comfortable as they talked, and she told Dan a rough outline of what had happened to her after the EMP. Before the event, she'd been a graduate student. She'd lived in university housing, not far from the main campus. She was one of the few students who'd actually understood the implications of what had happened. Everyone else, as she put it, was more than happy to stick their heads in the sand.

She'd barely been surviving by the time the soldiers picked her up. She'd been all alone. She'd convinced one friend to come with her, and they'd left campus together in an old vehicle that worked fine.

They'd lived for weeks on provisions taken from their campus dormitories, where they'd kept huge supplies of dried noodles, which they ate like crackers.

Olivia and her friend had had a few different run-ins, but none of them had turned violent until they'd encountered the soldiers. They'd shot her friend first without even asking any questions. Then they'd taken Olivia captive, and that was when Dan had first seen her.

Dan told her about the plan to get to Max's camp. He told her what he knew about Rob, which wasn't that much, and that Rob was coming with them.

"Do you think we can survive at this camp?"

"Yeah," said Dan. "If it's still there, I mean."

"They'll let us in? I mean, they'll accept us?"

"That's the sense I get, as long as we're willing to work. Do our share, and all that."

"That's never been a problem for me," said Olivia. "I'd be happy to have something to do, something to build. Everything seems like it's falling apart."

"I know what you mean," said Dan. "How are you feeling, anyway?"

"Better," said Olivia, glancing down at her wound. "I think your friend did a good job on my wound."

"And your ankle?"

She wiggled her foot around, moving it in all directions.

"Not great, but better. I'll try to see if I can walk on it soon."

"I don't think you broke it, so it should get better."

"Let's hope so."

Dan had found himself a seat on the floor, sitting cross-legged. To Dan's surprise, when he looked up the next time at Olivia she was smiling down at him, looking almost as if she was trying not to laugh at some joke.

"What's so funny?"

"Nothing," said Olivia, still smiling. "How old are you,

anyway?"

"Why?"

"Oh, I was just thinking how in our old world, I could be babysitting you, but you ended up saving my life. And now you're taking care of me."

"You saved my life, too," said Dan.

"I guess we're even then."

"Are you hungry?" said Dan, feeling for some reason that he wanted to change the course of the conversation.

"Starving," said Olivia. "But I don't suppose there's much food."

"That's where you're going to be surprised. We found all sorts of stuff here. It's incredible. But Rob's sleeping in the kitchen. I'll go in and bring you some stuff."

"Thanks."

Rob was snoring comfortably on the floor, still lying on his back. Dan tiptoed around him and gathered up a bunch of different foods. He made sure to get some tins of fish along with crackers and things like that. Olivia would need both protein and carbohydrate. The rest of the nutritional details didn't matter so much.

She was ecstatic to see the food when he brought it back, and she dug in immediately. Dan joined too, having grown hungry once again. He'd gone so long without really feeling full that his body was relishing the opportunity for more food, more calories, and more nutrients.

They ate together in silence.

"So you're supposed to wake up Rob for the next shift?" said Olivia, her mouth still partially full, a couple crackers in her hand.

Dan nodded.

"Why don't you two just sleep? I can do the next shift."

Dan shook his head. "You need to rest more than we

do," he said.

"I don't want to be a burden on everyone."

"It's going to be more a burden if you're still too weak to make the journey."

"Fair point. And how are we going to get there anyway?"

"Walking, unless we can find a vehicle."

"Where are we anyway?"

"Not really sure," said Dan. "But we need to go north-west in order to get to the hunting grounds where the camp is."

"And how far away do you think it'll take us?"

"Without knowing where we really are, it's hard to say."

Dan watched as Olivia set her food down and stood up slowly. She put the weight on her ankle slowly, treating it gingerly. Her face began showing pain, and soon she was wincing. But despite it, she did manage to stand on both her feet. She held her arms out as if she might lose her balance and fall down.

"You'd better sit back down," said Dan. "You don't want to overdo it."

"Just a minute longer. I know I can do it."

But soon the pain was too much, and she flopped back, exhausted, on the couch.

Neither of them said anything, but Dan knew they were thinking the same thing.

What would they do if she couldn't walk? Here she was, unable to stand up. There was no way she could walk all the way to the hunting grounds. It would take days, at a minimum.

But they couldn't abandon her. They couldn't just leave her there.

The silence hung heavy over the room.

"You two should just go without me," Olivia finally said.

Dan shook his head. "No," he said.

"Why not?"

"For one thing, you saved my life."

"You're just a kid," she said. "You deserve to get out of this madness if there's a chance for you."

Before Dan could respond there was a loud crack that came from outside the house.

Dan stood up, grabbing his gun.

Before he could make another move, Rob had already rushed into the room, eyes wide and alert, gun in his hand.

No one spoke for another thirty seconds. Rob and Dan moved to the windows, looking out through the blinds.

"Did it sound like it came from the front of the house to you, too?" Rob finally said.

Dan nodded.

There seemed to be nothing in the street. No cars, no people. Nothing.

There was another crack. Louder this time than before.

Dan couldn't identify the sound. It wasn't a gunshot. It wasn't thunder. The closest he could get was of some kind of material breaking, something stronger than wood, yet maybe more brittle.

"What do we do?" said Dan.

"We wait," said Rob. "Whatever's going on, what we know for sure is that there's someone out there. The last thing we need to do is rush out into the open where we'll be at a disadvantage. If they're dangerous, let them come to us."

The day had seemed to drag on and on. Physical work had never been something that Sadie had enjoyed before. In fact, she'd hated it. Before the EMP, she'd dreaded mowing the lawn and picking weeds.

It wasn't the work that made the day drag on. It was the worry. Her mother still wasn't back from her hunting trip.

Her mother had been a stickler for making sure her kids did their chores. And there hadn't been any talking her out of it. Sadie had pleaded with her mom, telling her that none of her friends at school had to mow the lawn at home, and that it was work for boys.

Of course, her mother wasn't having any of it. She'd divided the chores evenly between Sadie and James. She gave Sadie a little more slack than James because of her age, but didn't treat her any differently because she was a girl and James was a boy.

Since the EMP, Sadie had recognized the importance of what was going on. She'd understood the seriousness of the situation. She'd been happy to pitch in.

But she'd never, until today, really enjoyed physical work. It had always been a chore.

Now, she dove happily into the project of digging the ditches. It was something that helped her. It distracted her from the worry, from the worry about her mother, who still wasn't back from her hunting.

It also made her feel good. She relished the way her muscles felt, totally fatigued. She enjoyed the sweat dripping down from her brow.

It was as if she'd immersed herself back into the world, using her body as it was meant to be used. She was engaging with the physical world in a way that her pre-EMP world didn't let her.

Not only was the ditch a good distraction, but it could easily prove crucial to their very survival. It was a task with meaning and importance.

But the digging wasn't totally doing the trick. She was still worried.

"Don't you think we should go look for Mom?" said Sadie, pausing for a moment to turn to her brother.

"Not yet," said James.

"Aren't you worried about her?"

"Of course I am. But worrying doesn't do any good."

"But we could do something."

"Look at this way, Sadie," said James. "If she's in trouble, then she's already in trouble."

"That doesn't make any sense."

"What I mean is that she's either OK or she's not. If we leave now we'd be too late anyway."

"How could you say something like that?"

"I'm just trying to handle it my own way."

"You're a jerk."

"Let's not start this whole thing again."

"What whole thing?"

"The sibling bickering thing. We've got stuff to do."

Sadie sighed and went back to digging.

They'd made some progress with the ditches. They were all getting tired, but they were also getting better at digging. Sadie had noticed that certain ways of moving her body were more effective. She'd found her groove, so to speak, a way of moving that efficiently took dirt out from the ditches.

One problem they encountered was that the dirt had to go somewhere. They couldn't very well just pile it up next to the ditches they were digging. It'd be too obvious to someone approaching the camp that something was amiss.

Of course, the problem was alleviated somewhat by the fact that they'd decided not to dig the ditches as deep as they'd originally intended. They'd all been envisioning something that a person could actually fall completely into, immobilizing them, or injuring them with sharp sticks.

But if they'd wanted to dig a series of ditches that deep, it'd take weeks to get the project done, no matter how efficient they'd become in their digging technique. So instead they'd settled on something much more shallow.

The plan was to put sharp sticks in the sides. That might work. But if it didn't, a shallow ditch would be a good enough deterrent on its own. It'd be wide enough that it'd be hard not to step on it.

An enemy rolling an ankle would give those at the camp enough time to react. It'd give them the edge they needed.

At least that was the plan.

"All right, everybody," called out Cynthia, tossing aside her digging stone. "It's time for a break, right?"

"Not like there's a lot to snack on," said John.

"Whatever," said Cynthia, flopping herself down on the ground. "I'm beat. Food or not, I need a rest. Kids, come on, don't let this maniac work you to death."

"Just trying to keep us all alive," said John.

"Then don't work us to death in the process."

John laughed, and tossed his stone aside and went over to join Cynthia, motioning for Sadie and James to join them.

The four of them lay there on the ground spaced a few feet apart from each other. Sadie lay on her back and looked up at the sky.

The day felt much warmer than it had for a while. But it could just have been that her body temperature had risen from the work. Her empty stomach was growling at her. She was worried about her mother. But the day was nice.

Looking up at the sky, the trees formed a canopy. Their branches were bare, but soon there'd be leaves. Maybe times would get easier. Maybe living out here in nature would be nice. Once things calmed down, of course.

Sadie could imagine pleasant days during the summer. Maybe she'd really learn how to hunt. Her mother could teach her, and they could walk through the forest together, admiring the leaves and flowers.

But the nice thoughts started to fade almost as soon as they'd started. Her stomach was growling now, an intense rumbling of hunger.

"Isn't there anything to eat?" said Sadie. "I'm starving."

"We're all hungry, Sadie," said John. "But we've got to

save what we have until we really need it."

"This is when we need it. We can't do all this physical work and not eat."

"Like I said before, Sadie, we've..."

"Don't talk down to me like that," snapped Sadie, her mood suddenly turning for the worse. "I'm more than just some kid."

"Calm down, Sadie," said James.

"I've had enough of this," said Sadie, suddenly getting up and starting to walk away from them all.

"Sorry, John," James said. "Maybe it's her blood sugar or something. She can get grumpy when it gets low."

"It's not my blood sugar," snapped Sadie.

But maybe it was. She was only vaguely aware of how quickly her mood had shifted, but she did recognize that it had happened.

It wasn't just the lack of food. It was everything. All the stress. She could dream away about how nice things might be. But it didn't matter. The reality of their situation was harsh. Bleak and harsh.

Her mother hadn't come back.

And who knew what had happened to Max and Mandy. They might never hear from them again. And it wasn't like they'd read about it in the news later on, or get a postcard from them explaining what had happened.

No, it'd be nothing like that. It'd be nothing but silence, and they'd be left to speculate.

"You OK, Sadie?" called out Cynthia.

Sadie didn't answer. She just kept walking. She picked up her pace, and the next time she turned her head, she could no longer see the camp, the ditches, her brother, or John and Cynthia.

She needed to be alone.

17

Minutes had passed.

The dead man was right next to her. So was the dead deer. Blood stained the ground.

Georgia felt cold. The day might have been warm, but her body felt cold. Cold from hunger, cold from fear.

She thought of her children, of Sadie and James, back at camp.

She lay on her stomach. She'd crawled behind a tree. Only a part of her was exposed. Only her hands and head were a possible target.

She didn't dare get entirely behind the tree because it would give whoever was out there an opportunity to make a move without her knowing it.

It was a long-range standoff. The enemy was unknown, as was the outcome.

Her heart rate hadn't gone down. Her fingers felt freezing. Her feet did, too. It was the adrenaline. But she'd gone past the timeframe when it had pumped her up, readied her for action.

Now she just felt its negative effects. She felt the cold and the fear. She felt the worry, the anxiety rushing through her like a tidal wave.

How could she possibly get out of this alive?

She needed to talk herself through it.

She could outshoot many. She had experience. She knew what she was doing. Whoever was out there had already taken some shots at her. And they'd missed.

She couldn't count on them missing again.

But she did know that she wouldn't miss.

Her rifle was ready.

Her eye was pressed to the scope. She was ready. As ready as she'd ever be.

There was movement off in the distance, near a cluster of trees.

Nothing but a flash of something. Clothing, or a sneaker maybe. Something reflective. Maybe camping gear.

Georgia moved her eye away from the scope to check her surroundings. But just for a moment.

Then she was back at it. She hadn't moved her gun. She was honed in on the place where she'd glimpsed the movement.

Now there was someone there, practically right in the crosshairs.

It was a man, short and plump. He held a rifle.

Georgia didn't bother studying him. She didn't bother taking a second look. She'd already recognized that he wasn't one of her own. She'd already recognized that he was the one who'd been firing at her.

She took aim.

She pulled the trigger.

The gun kicked.

It was a clean shot.

Right in the heart.

The man fell to the ground.

Georgia waited, the gunshot ringing in her ears.

She stayed there, pressed to the ground, for a full ten minutes before moving. She used the scope to check on the dead man, to scout the area, and she also made sure to check her surroundings.

There wasn't any movement. There wasn't anything out there.

Or if there was someone out there, they were staying still. Very still.

She couldn't stay there forever. Most likely, that had been it. Just two men. Nothing more.

Georgia stood up slowly. Her body felt weak.

She'd have liked to check the dead man. His gun would be useful, as well as his ammunition and anything else he had on him. She'd have liked to check Baxter as well, the other dead man.

She'd also have liked to try to find their camp, to see if they were the ones who'd stolen the food.

She would have really liked to start processing the deer, bringing some of the meat back to camp.

But her legs were wobbly. Her injury was hurting her. Her vision was going blurry with fatigue. She wondered if she could make it back to camp at all in her state.

It was hard for her to admit that she couldn't accomplish something. Especially something physical.

But she wasn't going to let that kill her off. She couldn't exhaust herself and succumb to some bad fate out here. Not when her kids needed her.

So she started off, ignoring everything that needed to be done. Her focus became simply getting back to camp.

She walked slowly but at a steady pace. She didn't want to exhaust herself anymore.

It'd take a couple hours to get back at the rate she was going. She stopped only once, to make herself a makeshift staff from a piece of wood. It made the going a little easier, and she found herself leaning on it more and more the farther along she went.

She took a more direct route back towards the camp than she had when she'd been heading out. On the way out, she'd been hoping to catch a deer somewhere along the way. Now, she just wanted to get back.

When she was about a half hour away from the camp, she saw something that made her pause.

It was an empty plastic bottle. It looked like a milk jug. A gallon. Crumpled and lying on the ground.

She stood there, perfectly still, staring at it.

What was it doing out here? She knew it hadn't come from her camp.

A noise in the distance sent her heart thumping again in her chest. It was the sound of a human voice.

Many human voices.

They were shouting. Some were laughing. But it wasn't real laughter. It was crazed, high-pitched laughter that sent a chill through her exhausted body.

There was no question in Georgia's mind about what it was.

It was the mob.

Or another one.

But they were all the same.

They acted the same way. They "thought" the same way, if you could even call it that.

She'd thought they were done with the roving groups

of desperate people. They'd defeated them last time, hanging on to their lives and their camp, but just barely.

Now another mob was back. And close to their camp.

Georgia didn't even blink. She just continued, picking up her pace, ignoring her protesting body.

She needed to get back as soon as possible. She needed to warn the others.

They needed to prepare.

18

DAN

The three of them waited in silence as the sounds continued.

"It sounds like wood breaking," whispered Olivia finally.

Rob nodded. "Someone's breaking into a house."

Dan felt his breathing go a little easier, a little more relaxed. They weren't in the clear, but at least it wasn't their house that was being broken into.

They were safe. At least for the moment.

Suddenly, Rob broke from his frozen pose and became a flurry of quick movement. He was rushing around the room, grabbing his pack, checking his gun.

"Come on," he said. "Now's our chance."

"What are you talking about?" said Dan.

"We've got to go."

"Go? Now? We know someone's out there."

"Exactly," said Rob. "And there's a chance that they came here in a vehicle. Now's our chance to take it."

"That's really risky," said Dan.

"Yeah, it's risky. But so is having to walk north to your friend's camp."

Dan didn't know what to do. The thought of heading outside into certain danger sent chills down his spine.

But he saw Rob looking pointedly at Olivia, and Dan understood the message. There was no way Olivia was going to make it on foot up north. It was a vehicle or nothing. And they couldn't leave her behind.

"But we don't even know they have a car or anything," said Dan. "How likely do you think it is?"

Rob shrugged. "It's worth a chance." He said it casually, as if he were discussing the weather.

"Don't you think we could start out walking and pick up a vehicle somewhere else?"

Rob shook his head. "They're getting rarer. The ones that work, at least. Trust me, I've been all over this area. You don't come across working vehicles that often now. If they're working, they're in hiding. Those who have them understand how valuable they are."

"Fine," muttered Dan. "It's worth a look, I guess."

"Good choice, kid," said Rob, handing Dan a loaded gun.

"Don't go out there," said Olivia, looking up at both of them from the couch. "Don't go out on account of me. You've already done so much for me."

"I guess we haven't really been introduced," said Rob, cracking a smile and holding out a hand for her to shake.

She looked up at it, confused, before shaking it gently.

"It's not really up to you to decide," said Rob.

"Yeah," said Olivia. "But Dan's just a kid. He can't keep risking his life for me."

"You saved my life," said Dan.

"And he's not a kid any longer," said Rob. "That's the

new world we're living in. There's no sheltering anyone these days. Come on, kid."

Rob led the way, out of the room and towards the hallway.

"Dan," said Olivia, before Dan was all the way out of the room. "You don't have to do this."

Dan said nothing because he didn't know what to say.

He clutched the handgun tightly. The safety was off. His finger was on the trigger.

Rob had his hand on the handle of the front door.

"We're going out the front door?" whispered Dan, surprised.

"What better way than to gain the element of surprise?" said Rob, a half-smile forming on his lips.

Rob opened the door in one swift motion. The dim afternoon light flooded inside.

Dan looked up at Rob, who stood there, big and tall. His shoulders were wide and he held his gun in both hands. He looked impossibly tough, the last sort of person you'd want to mess with. Dan was glad he was on his side.

Rob stepped outside, brushing the screen door away like a gnat.

Dan followed. He squinted against the light.

They both looked around. There was nothing in sight. Nothing but houses close together and the narrow street.

"You hear an engine anywhere?"

Dan shook his head.

"They've probably got it turned off. We've got to find the source of the sound."

The cracking sound came to them again. Louder this time, now that they were outdoors.

Dan cocked his head. "Sounds like it's over that way,"

he said, pointing in front of them, up the street. It was probably north, but he wasn't sure.

"Let's go. Stay a couple steps behind me, to my right. I need to know where you are."

Dan nodded, and they set off, walking through the small yards of the houses, staying as far away from the road as possible. There wasn't really any way to camouflage themselves, to remain hidden while moving, but at least they weren't right in the middle of the road.

Still, they were targets.

The sounds continued. Dan could hear the tone of it more clearly now. It might have been wood breaking, or it might have been something else. What the hell were they doing? Breaking a house down piece by piece? Stealing the siding off of it?

It didn't make sense, but Dan guessed that it didn't have to. All they needed was a vehicle.

But it seemed like a long shot. Why did Rob think they'd have one? It was nothing more than a guess.

And a risky guess at that.

They walked down to the next intersection, took a right, continued for a little ways, and then took a left.

The sound was getting louder.

"Sounds like they're doing home renovations," joked Rob.

Dan was too nervous to laugh. It didn't seem like the time for jokes to him. His heart was beating fast and beads of sweat formed on his forehead. He was clutching the gun so tightly that his knuckles were turning white and his fingers hurt.

"You know how to use that thing, right, kid?" said Rob, glancing back at Dan and his gun.

"Uh, for the most part," said Dan.

"You've got the safety off. That's a good start. Just point and shoot. Not much to it."

Dan knew there was a lot more to it than that, and the knowledge didn't make him feel any more confident.

The street they were on ended only a few houses down. There wasn't a cul-de-sac. It wasn't that type of neighborhood. The street simply dumped out into a tiny lot filled with refuse, discard and rusted shopping carts. Plastic bags lay here and there, some of them blowing in the wind.

There was a car parked in front of a small blue house. It was the only one on the street, and it was parked in the middle of the road.

It was one of those boxy Chevrolets from the early 1980s. The paint was dinged up and there were dents all over the roof.

The sounds were louder.

"Sounds like they're coming from around back," said Rob. "That must be the car. Come on."

Dan's heart was beating faster than ever.

Rob broke into a jog, and Dan picked up his own pace. They were only two houses away from the car now. They were closing the distance. Still no sign of whoever was making those sounds.

"Get in," said Rob, when they reached the car. He threw open the driver's side door and threw himself into the seat.

The passenger side door was locked.

Rob reached over and unlocked it from the inside. Dan opened it. The hinges were rusty and it swung unevenly, but Dan got the heavy door opened, got himself inside, and tried to close it quietly.

But despite his efforts, the door slammed closed. It was just too heavy.

Shit. Would they hear it?

There was a pause in the snapping sounds coming from behind the house.

Rob was frantically searching the interior for the keys. "They've got to be here somewhere," he said. "Help me look."

Dan opened the glove box, which was half-broken, and everything immediately fell out onto the floor at his feet. There were old food wrappers that smelled, insurance paperwork, and a huge cluster of keys on a big ring, like the type a janitor would carry on the job.

"Pass me those," said Rob.

Another snapping sound. Loud. So they hadn't heard the door slamming.

"Don't you think they'd have taken the keys with them?" said Dan.

Rob had the big key ring in his hands, and was flipping through the keys rapidly, one by one. Some of them were huge, and obviously didn't go to a car. Some looked like house keys. Some were rusted. Some were filthy.

Rob tried the most promising ones one by one.

"They probably did," said Rob. "But maybe there's a spare here."

"Maybe they kept one under the car," said Dan. "You know, one of those little magnetic compartments?"

"Good call," said Rob. "Get out and look for it."

Dan opened the car door again, wishing he'd thought of it earlier. He had to push with all his weight to get the door opened enough to squeeze out.

Dan ran his hand underneath the filthy car, searching

with his hand. He was down on his hands and knees when he heard a gunshot.

The shot rang out.

The passenger window above Dan's head shattered. The bullet had struck it, pierced it, and left a small hole surrounded by a spider-web of hairline fractures.

"Rob!"

Had he been hit?

The old car suddenly roared to a start.

"In the car!" shouted Rob.

If Rob had been hit, he was still alive enough to turn on the car.

Dan turned his head to see two figures coming down the driveway. One held a handgun. The other swung a baseball bat at his side.

They were closing the distance fast.

As Dan rose to get into the car, he pointed his handgun and squeezed the trigger three times in quick succession. The gun kicked more than he'd been expecting. He didn't hit them. His aim was way off, but it made them take cover.

The two men threw themselves to the ground just as Dan threw himself onto the passenger's seat.

Rob already had the car in reverse. He hit the gas the second Dan was in the car.

The engine roared. The tires squealed.

The car jerked back a foot then suddenly stopped.

Rubber was burning. The strong stench of it billowed into the air along with smoke.

Dan's head whiplashed into the seat's padded headrest.

The emergency brake was on. Rob found the release with his left hand and undid it.

The car rocketed backwards, roaring backwards down the street, leaving a cloud of rubber smoke behind it.

The two men were in the middle of the street, sprinting towards the car.

When they reached the cross street, Rob swung the wheel hard. The car spun around sharply.

The back bumper slammed into a streetlight, making a horrendous crunching sound.

Dan was thrown back once again.

Rob jerked the shifter into drive, and they were off again.

The tires spun and squealed, and they were speeding down the streets they'd just walked down.

"They still coming for us?" shouted Rob over the roar of the engine.

Dan checked the back window.

"Yeah," he yelled.

"We're going to have to be quick about this. We've got to get Olivia and all the gear. We're not going to have much of a head start on them. They'll be coming for us."

"What about the food?"

"I packed most of it away. Now Olivia can't walk. I'm going to have to go get her."

"I can..."

"You can't carry her quickly enough. You're going to have to stay outside and fend them off if they get close."

Dan gulped down the fear he felt creeping up from his chest into his throat.

They were barreling down the street towards the house where Olivia rested in the living room.

"Which one is it?"

"Right there!"

Rob slammed on the brakes. The car rocked to a violent stop.

Rob had the door opened before Dan could say anything. He was already dashing across the lawn towards the front door.

Dan glanced nervously back through the windshield.

There wasn't anyone there. The road was empty. But they'd be coming. He just hoped that Rob would be back out of the house with Olivia before they got there.

How could he fight them off by himself?

But if he had to, he was going to be ready. Gun in hand, he opened the door, shoving his weight against it.

He got into position in front of the hood of the car. It'd give him some cover, and he'd still be able to see them coming.

Dan glanced back at the house, the screen door still creaking on its hinges. The seconds were ticking by. Rob needed to hurry up.

A thought crossed through his mind. Was it right, what they'd just done? They'd stolen the car from two strangers. They didn't know anything about them. They didn't know what kind of people they were, or what they'd been doing by making those strange noises.

And if they came for the car, Dan would only have one choice. He'd have to shoot. Shoot to kill if he could.

It didn't seem right.

But he couldn't let that stop him.

After all, he had been shot at. They'd opened fire first.

Of course, they'd had good reason. Their car'd been stolen.

"I just can't get it out of my head," said Mandy. "It's just so weird."

Max just grunted, saying nothing.

"What do you think they were doing with them? Eating them? Fattening them up and eating them one by one?"

"Doesn't sound very efficient," said Max. His voice sounded hoarse and tired. His face looked drained of its energy.

"You feeling OK?" said Mandy. "You don't look so good."

"I'm fine," grunted Max.

"Your leg OK?"

He grunted again, giving a stiff nod.

They'd been walking for a full day. They'd decided they wanted to get back as quickly as possible. Any time they stopped to rest, they'd be exposing themselves to more danger. And they'd have to take turns sleeping in case anything happened.

They knew from experience that taking turns sleeping only led to both of them being semi-exhausted rather than fully rested.

So they'd decided to press on, as far as they could. It was all a gamble. Exhaustion made them less able to fight.

But since they didn't know what the odds were, they were guessing as best they could.

Nothing could be perfect. Not since the EMP.

Mandy had been feeling all right. She'd been on her second or third wind for the last couple hours. She'd lost track.

But now the exhaustion hit her like a ton of bricks. She felt it in her muscles, and deep in her bones.

She was out of breath. And all of a sudden.

"You'd better eat something," said Max, who must have been passing through the states of exhaustion at a different rate than she was. He was going slow and steady. "Here." He handed her a bag of chips.

"Jerky?" she panted.

"You need the carbohydrate now," said Max. "Trust me."

As they walked, Mandy tried to open the bag of chips with her hands, but she soon gave up, handing the bag to Max, who opened it for her.

The chips tasted good. The salt was the best part of them.

A few minutes after eating the chips, and drinking a healthy amount of soda, Mandy started to feel a little better.

"Maybe I'm hitting my fourth wind," she said. "Do those exist?"

"Why not?" said Max.

They were walking north. They'd left the highways behind and were walking on rural roads. They'd passed alongside a few small towns. They'd walked through old industrial areas, where the factories had closed down years before the EMP.

They'd walked by train tracks and small rivers.

They hadn't seen anyone. Not a single car or a face. Part of that was because they'd kept their distance.

"You think everyone's dead or in hiding?" said Mandy.

"A little bit of both," said Max.

"You OK?"

"Yeah," he grunted. "It's just my leg."

"You want to stop and rest?"

He shook his head. "I can keep going. Any idea how close we are?"

Mandy had been thinking about their position for the entire trip, and while she didn't know precisely where they were, she had a vague enough idea.

"Maybe one day more," she said. "We're not going to be able to walk straight through."

Mad nodded. "Let's keep going through the night, though," he said.

Their conversation grew sparser as the day turned into night and the serious fatigue set in. Mandy had gotten far past any third or fourth winds.

She'd gotten to the point where she had to actively concentrate on putting one foot in front of the other. It was like consciously sending messages to her body to keep moving.

If something happened, if someone came along and they had to fight, she knew she wouldn't be any good.

But they pressed on, hoping that the cover of darkness

would help them. Mandy had rubbed dirt on her sneakers, and Max had cut the reflective pieces off with his knife.

They had no packs, and no flashlights either. It was hard to see at times, but their eyes adjusted somewhat. It'd be hard to spot them unless someone really knew where to look.

The darkness was, at times, so intense that Mandy found herself engulfed in terror. Before the EMP, the night had always been something that had frightened her. First, as a child, she'd been scared of the usual monsters under the bed and the unknown that the yawning blackness offered.

Later, as an adult, it had been a matter of practicality. Night was when people got mugged and attacked.

She was trying to remind herself that the night was to their advantage now.

But it didn't quite work.

Her rational mind knew that the night now offered more serious threats than before the EMP. After all, she'd lived in a relatively safe area with little crime. And the monsters from her childhood had never even been real.

Somehow, they managed to trudge through the entire night, and when the sun rose, they found themselves standing on the side of a familiar road.

"This'll take us back to camp," said Mandy. They were the first words either of them had spoken in hours.

"You sure?"

Mandy nodded. "I don't know how it happened, but somehow we're back on that road..."

But she couldn't remember the name of it. Max seemed to understand, and didn't ask her. He must have trusted her. Maybe as much as she trusted him.

"We're going to make it," said Max.

He put his arm around her back and pulled her close. They stood there together on the edge of the empty road with the sun rising.

John was the one who saw Georgia first.

She looked beyond exhausted. Her face had gone completely pale.

His first reaction was to grab his rifle and point it in her direction. After all, the way things had been going, there could easily be trouble. People behind her. People following her. Anything was possible.

He waited for Georgia to call out, for her to tell him that everything was clear.

But she said nothing.

He walked forward slowly, keeping his eyes trained on the surroundings rather than Georgia.

But there was nothing.

When he got to her, he gave her his arm.

"You OK?"

She nodded.

But she didn't seem OK.

"Anyone follow you?"

"Don't know."

"Let's get you back to the van. Are you injured?"

She shook her head.

She leaned most of her weight against him and together they limped back to the van.

Sadie, James, and Cynthia came running over.

"Mom, are you all right?"

"I'm fine, kids."

"Get her some water. And something to eat."

"Exactly what food are you talking about?" said Cynthia.

"Just get something," snapped John.

There was food and Cynthia knew it. Just not a lot of it.

When Cynthia came back with some water and a can of tuna fish, Georgia started to feel a little better.

"What happened, Georgia?"

Before she would tell them what had happened, she ordered her kids and Cynthia to get back on watch duty. "And be careful," she added. "There's another mob out there."

"Are they headed this direction?"

"Just get out there. We can't all be here in the van, relaxing."

John let out a little laugh. "Well, you heard her."

James and Sadie seemed reluctant to leave their mother's side, but they agreed, grabbed their rifles, and set off with Cynthia.

Georgia began to tell John the whole story, how she'd run into those two men, and how her old injuries had gotten the best of her.

"They're not exactly that old. You're trying to do too much, that's all. You're going to be fine."

"I know I'm going to be fine," said Georgia. Her voice had come back, almost to full strength. "But there's a deer out there that I left. And there's another huge mob of people."

"How many?"

"Don't know."

"You think they're coming this direction?"

"Really no way to know. But if they're looking for something, they'll end up here."

"Why's that?"

"We've got weapons. Some food. They're desperate."

John said nothing for a moment. He was running through the possibilities in his head.

"Well," he finally said. "We got through it last time."

"Just barely," said Georgia.

"I wish Max and Mandy were back."

"Me too."

He told her about the ditches. They'd gotten about halfway done encircling the camp.

"You think they'll be effective against a big group of desperate people?"

"They'll do something. Sounds like we were digging in the wrong place, though." He pointed to the other side of the camp, where'd they'd done most of the digging.

They hadn't even broken earth on the side of camp that Georgia had come from, where the mob was most likely to come from.

"Well," said Georgia, sitting up from the seat she'd been reclining in. "We've got work to do, that's all."

She was already trying to get up, with one hand holding onto the above-door handle, trying to pull herself out of the van.

"You're crazy, Georgia," muttered John, grabbing her by the sides and restraining her. "We'll do it. You rest."

"I can't sit back and watch everyone else work."

"That's fair. But give it half an hour, OK?"

"All right, fine. Half an hour. I'll be as good as new."

"I don't doubt that." He took binoculars that he'd been carrying around his neck and handed them to her. "We're going to need a good lookout if we're all going to be digging."

John was tired and hungry, but not too far gone to do some more work. He shook his fatigued arms as they hung at his sides, trying to get his muscles to loosen up.

With James's help, he marked out a line that they could dig along.

"Is my mom going to be OK?" said James.

"She's going to be fine, yeah. She's tougher than she looks."

"You don't need to tell me that."

John laughed as much as he could. There was something about exhaustion and hunger that sapped the laughter right out of someone.

It was a shame they couldn't get that deer. They desperately all needed a good meal. A lot of protein, and plenty of fat.

John could almost taste the venison in his mouth. What he craved most of all was the fat, the delicious hot gristle, roasted over the campfire, that melted in your mouth.

There wasn't anything to do but dig. And dig some more.

They kept going. John tried to set an example of going at a slow and steady pace. After all, James and Sadie were just kids. They needed someone to look up to, to follow. Cynthia was pulling her own weight, but she wasn't always the best example. She had, as John knew well, a tendency to run her mouth, to make sarcastic remarks, and to complain when it suited her, without considering how it might affect the morale of everyone else.

"Hey!" shouted Georgia, out of nowhere.

John glanced back over his shoulder to see Georgia waving at him from where she sat in the open door of the van. He groaned. He wished that she hadn't moved herself from the relative comfort of the van seat.

"What is it?"

"There's someone out there!"

Georgia had dropped the binoculars back around her neck in favor of her rifle. Her eye was pressed to the scope.

James, Sadie, and Cynthia had already grabbed their rifles.

John took his from where he'd had it strapped to his back. It felt good to have it again in his hands.

But it didn't feel good to know that someone was out there.

"Get back," hissed John in a voice that was both a whisper and a command.

John didn't see anything out there in the woods. It looked as it always had. Leafless trees. The ground. The sky.

It was all normal.

Then he saw it. A flash of movement.

A torn white t-shirt off in the distance. Heading towards them.

John wasn't going to take any chances. Not this time.

The way he saw it, he was done with asking questions first and getting shot at second. If he kept doing that, he'd wind up dead before long. It was a surprise he wasn't dead already.

The way John saw it, if someone was approaching the camp, then it was their responsibility to announce themselves, to declare themselves innocent, to put down their weapons and approach with their hands up.

He'd grown harsher, yes. But that was the way it was.

He already knew there was another mob out there.

John got the white shirt in his sights. It belonged to a tall, lanky man. He was unkempt. A patchy beard and long hair. He was smeared with dirt.

And he was coming towards them.

John pulled the trigger. The rifle kicked. The shot rang out.

The white-shirted man didn't fall.

He'd been shot in the shoulder. A splotch of blood appeared there, but the man continued to stagger forward.

Before John could get off another shot, another rifle rang out. Then another. And another.

The white-shirt man crumpled to the ground. His chest had become pockmarked with bullet holes.

The gunshots faded away into deafening silence. No one spoke.

John waited, not moving.

He knew that if there were others, the gunshots would only attract them. To a group of people who had become so desperate that they'd lost their individuality completely, gunshots didn't mean danger. To them, gunshots meant opportunity. It meant a chance to swarm, to find food, to find supplies, a chance to grasp at the possibility of living another day.

Sure enough, another person appeared. A woman. Off in the distance.

Then another. A man.

Then another.

And another.

It was happening.

John hoped they could hold them off this time.

They'd barely made it last time. And they'd been comparatively well-fed. Comparatively rested.

This was going to be tough.

21

DAN

D an saw them coming running down the road, brandishing their weapons and yelling.

Dan glanced back at the house. Still no movement. What was taking Rob so long?

Dan didn't have much time. He'd been found, and the men would close the distance fast.

Even if Rob appeared at the door with Olivia in the next five seconds, it still wouldn't be enough time to get away without a fight.

Rob would be burdened down carrying Olivia and the gear. He wouldn't be any use in a fight like that.

It was up to Dan.

And Dan alone.

Dan ducked down behind the car, hoping they hadn't seen him at all.

He could hear their shoes slapping against the pavement. They were close. Very close now.

Dan started counting the seconds in his head.

One Mississippi...

He had a plan. When he got to the count of five, he'd pop his head up and start shooting.

But he didn't want to go through with it. Every fiber of his body was screaming out, telling him not to do it, telling him it was a terrible idea.

And it was a terrible idea.

Waiting until they got close enough to actually hit him? And then exposing himself?

But it was the only thing he could think of. He knew that with his inexperience, he didn't have a chance at hitting the men from any real distance. He needed them to be close.

Two Mississippi...

An idea popped into Dan's head.

Another plan.

He was small. Short and skinny. He could use it to his advantage.

Without thinking, he threw himself down onto the pavement, facedown. He did it too fast, and his nose bashed against the hard surface.

It began bleeding, blood dripping down. But he ignored it.

There was just enough space underneath the car for Dan to get under it.

With gun in hand, he squeezed himself all the way underneath the car.

Three Mississippi...

He kept crawling, his elbows and face occasionally scraping the rough pavement. He knocked his head against the car.

He ignored it all and kept going.

Four Mississippi...

There wasn't much time.

He could see their legs out from the other side of the car.

They were getting close.

If he didn't make the shot, he'd be stuck underneath the car. If Rob and Olivia came out of the house at the wrong moment, they'd be completely exposed and completely undefended.

Five.

Dan had his arms stretched straight out, gun in both hands. He took aim as best he could, lining it all up.

He squeezed the trigger. The gun kicked harder than he'd been expecting. The sound was defending, reverberating in the small area underneath the car. His ears rang in pain.

A scream.

One of the men collapsed to the ground.

Dan had hit him in the shin.

It was strange seeing him fall from the limited viewpoint that Dan had.

The scream of pain didn't end. It continued, on and on.

Dan wasted no time.

The other pair of legs were dancing around. The other man was probably trying to find where the shooter was.

Dan squeezed the trigger.

The gun kicked.

He missed.

"Get him!" the fallen man was yelling.

Dan pulled the trigger again.

He missed again.

He pulled the trigger yet another time.

But nothing happened.

Was it jammed?

He didn't know. He didn't know enough about guns.

The only thing he knew was that it wasn't going to work. He needed another weapon.

As fast as he could, he scuttled sideways. He needed to get out from underneath the car.

The man whose shin he'd shot was lying on the ground screaming in pain. He faced away from Dan. He was the one with the gun.

That meant that the man Dan hadn't gotten was the one with the baseball bat.

That was good. Dan figured he had a better shot against a baseball bat than a gun.

Dan's armed scraped painfully against the pavement. He was moving too fast. His forearm, exposed, was bleeding.

Before he could get out from under the car, the man he'd shot suddenly flipped himself around. Now he was staring face to face with Dan. They were both on the same level.

"He's there! Under the car."

Dan saw the gun pointing towards him.

But there wasn't anything he could do other than keep going.

A shot rang out.

It missed, piercing some part of the car.

Dan was suddenly out from underneath the vehicle.

He scrambled to his feet, still holding the gun that might have been jammed.

He was out of view of the man with the gun. But his feet weren't.

If Dan wasn't careful, he might get his own shin shot.

"Dan!"

Rob had appeared at the doorway to the house. Olivia

was slung over his shoulder and he held onto her with one arm. The pack was strapped to his back. In his free arm, he held a handgun.

A shot rang out.

The screaming man fell silent. Hopefully he was dead, and Dan wouldn't have to worry about his shins.

It was all happening so fast.

A flurry of movement.

The baseball bat was speeding towards his head. He hadn't even seen the man who wielded it appear.

It was a good swing. Fast and intense and powerful.

Dan brought up both his hands as fast as he could, trying to shield himself.

But it wasn't enough. The bat knocked through the flimsy shield of his comparatively weak hands and smashed right into his face.

Pain flared through him. Blood was pouring from somewhere. He tasted it in his mouth.

Dan brought up his hands again. It was purely instinctual.

He was on the ground, and the baseball bat was coming down hard again towards him.

A series of gunshots rang out. Dan didn't know how many.

The man let out a strange, muted noise. Something between a moan of pain and a scream.

He fell right on top of Dan.

Dan lay there, trying to breathe, the pain in his face overwhelming him. Blood from the corpse mixed with his own. The weight of the man was crushing him.

"You still with us, kid?" came Rob's deep voice.

The next thing knew, the dead body was pulled off

him, and Rob was standing there, offering him a strong hand.

Dan took it, and Rob pulled him to his feet.

"You don't look too bad," he said, winking at him. "You'll be all right. Come on, get in the car. There isn't much time. We've probably attracted every scrounger and idiot in the area."

Using his sleeve, Dan wiped the blood from his face as best he could. But it kept coming. His face was painful and sore to the touch. He stumbled around the front or back of the car, he wasn't sure which. He made it through one of the open doors and collapsed onto one of the seats.

"Olivia?" said Dan, his voice sounding funny. Maybe his lips were swollen.

"She's fine. Right, Olivia?"

"Never been better," came Olivia's voice.

"You did good, kid. Now let's get the hell out of here."

Dan wiped away more blood. Now he could see again. Rob was in the front seat and Dan and Olivia were in the back.

Rob twisted the key in the ignition.

The car started and Dan felt it start to speed away.

"What took you so long?" Dan managed to say.

"You know how these things go," said Rob. "Packing for a trip always takes longer than you'd think."

"It was my fault," said Olivia. "I'm sorry, Dan."

Dan wondered what she'd meant, but she didn't elaborate, and he didn't ask.

He was alive. That was what was important. No matter how bad his injuries were, they'd heal with time.

They drove in silence. Rob seemed to know the streets well, and he seemed comfortable taking the various turns.

The streets were narrow and the houses remained close together.

Dan looked out through the windows. He was sure that his eye was black, and he could feel the swelling already starting. But he could still see well enough.

There was no one out there. To be seen, at least. Those who were out there were in hiding.

In this area, at least, the battles were raging mostly behind closed doors. Those who remained were still fighting for their lives, but they were doing it mostly in private.

Dan remembered back to when he'd been holed up in his grandfather's house, anxiously waiting for someone to break in, for something to happen.

Those who'd remained in their homes would be in the same position now. Only worse. Food was only getting scarcer. And people were only getting more desperate.

How would it end? What would be the final outcome to those who hadn't fled?

No one was coming to help. That much was certain at this point.

And no new communities seemed to be developing. At least not here. Not yet.

Instead, it was just a further breakdown of society. More tears in the social fabric.

Violent tears.

"How you two doing?" said Rob, from the front.

"Not bad," said Dan.

"Olivia?"

"I'm glad to get out of there, but do you really think we can get all the way to this campground?"

"Let's hope so," said Rob. "If this car will make it, then I think we have a good chance."

"What if we run into someone?"

"We'll just have to take it off the cuff, as they say."

The three of them fell silent, and the drive continued. The houses grew further and further apart, and soon they were out on the open road.

Rob took them down back roads, rather than the highway. He seemed to know them well.

Night fell, and they drove on. Rob didn't use the headlights unless it was absolutely necessary. It was better not to call too much attention to themselves.

Olivia fell asleep at some point, and her slight snores echoed through the noisy car. Rob pushed the car onward, driving as fast as he could without the lights.

Dan stayed awake the whole way. The pain, for one thing, didn't let him go to sleep.

And his mind was active. If the camp was still there, if Max was still alive, what would his new life be like?

Maybe it'd be a new life, full of peace, free of worry. At least as free of worry as a post-EMP life could be.

"I can't believe we're almost back," said Mandy. "I just can't believe we're here."

Max nodded.

He agreed. It was strange to find themselves back on the hunting grounds. He almost couldn't believe that they'd made it.

If it hadn't been for Mandy's unusually good sense of direction and memory for landmarks, Max didn't think they would have gotten there. It wasn't that he had a bad memory for those things, just that Mandy's was superb.

"You think they missed us?" said Mandy.

"I just hope they're still alive," said Max.

"This was a lot easier driving out of than walking into," said Mandy as they set off down the access road that they'd driven the pickup down not so long ago.

"I'm just happy we're still walking."

"Always the optimist."

Max found himself smiling. A brief smile, but a smile nevertheless.

"Did I just see you smile?" said Mandy. "You got my joke?"

"Maybe I'm happy to be back."

"I don't think I've ever heard you say you were happy."

"There hasn't been much to be happy about."

"Except for being able to walk. And not lying injured or dead in a ditch somewhere."

"Sometimes I wonder how we even did it."

"That makes two of us."

It was a couple more hours of walking back to the camp.

"Well," said Mandy, pausing. The van and the tent were in view. "Here we are."

"Come on," said Max, leading the way.

"I was waiting for you to say that we need to get to work," said Mandy.

Max gave a tired laugh. "I think we both need a rest. We'll start work tomorrow."

It was early in the morning. Everyone would most likely be asleep, except for whoever was on guard duty.

But he didn't see anyone. Maybe they were hiding. Maybe they'd found a new spot to watch from.

"Stop!" shouted someone, frantically. "Don't take another step!"

Max and Mandy froze.

"James?" called out Mandy. "Is that you? It's us."

Sure enough, it was James. He emerged from behind a tree on the other side of camp. He carried a rifle, and looked thinner than when they'd left.

Mandy started to walk forward.

"Stop!" called out James again. "I'm serious!"

Mandy froze.

"I thought you'd be happy to see us!"

"There's a trap," called out James, walking towards them.

Max was already looking around. His eyes settled on the ground, where it looked like dead leaves had been rearranged to cover up something.

"A ditch?" said Max.

"Yeah," said James.

"Good work," said Max.

"Well, it's not that deep. It's harder to dig than we thought."

"I thought you were bringing someone back with you," said James.

"It didn't work out," said Max.

The reunion didn't quite have the same tone that reunions did before the EMP, like when families would meet each other at the airport arrival gates.

Things remained subdued even as everyone woke up and came sleepily out of the van and the tent.

They were happy to see Max and Mandy, of course, but Max soon learned just how rough a time they'd had of it while they were gone.

There'd been a huge band of chaotic people, acting as a mob, that had attacked them not long ago. And then another smaller one just a couple days ago.

For some reason, the second mob had been scared off. But they were still out there, somewhere nearby in the woods.

Georgia was doing better, but she'd recently pushed herself too hard. She looked OK now to Max, but he could still see that something was hurting her. He recognized the look in her face when the injury was acting up. He knew it well, since his leg still bothered him.

They'd gone hungry. And only yesterday they'd made

the dangerous trip past the gathering mob to the deer that Georgia had seen shot just a couple days ago. They'd managed to drag it back to camp.

"You wouldn't still have some of that deer lying around, would you, by any chance?" said Mandy, trying to make a joke out of it.

"Sure," said John. "You two must be starving."

Half an hour later, they were all sitting around the smoldering campfire eating venison and drinking coffee with sugar.

Max and Mandy handed out a couple of the bags of chips that they still had left. They'd already drank all the soda, but some of the flavors weren't to their likings, despite their hunger.

But John and James, it turned out, loved jalapeño flavored chips, no matter how spicy they were.

"So tell me more about this mob," said Max. "You've already been attacked? Tell me exactly what happened."

"We survived," said Georgia.

"But it's not the end," said Cynthia. "Don't worry, they're still out there."

"How many?"

"A couple dozen. More than before."

"But they're not moving," said Mandy. "Maybe they're just going to stay in one place. Why do you think they'll attack?"

"Because they're probing," said John. "Small groups of a couple of them are coming our way. We do what we can, but some of them inevitably escape. And presumably they report back."

"I thought you said they were acting more like animals than people?" said Mandy.

"In a sense, yes."

"You're talking about this mob as if it's an entirely different organism."

"Humanity at its worst," muttered Max.

"Hey, Max, can I talk to you for a second?" said John, standing up and nodding over to an area away from the campfire.

Max nodded and joined his brother.

When they were out of earshot from the campfire, Max said, "what's up?"

"I'm worried," said John. "You came back at the best time for us, but the worst time for you and Mandy."

"It sounds like you don't think we're going to make it through this."

"I don't want to worry everyone else. It's just going to bring morale down and decrease their ability to fight."

"They're adults," said Max. "They can take the news. I don't think it's a good idea to mislead anyone."

"They're not all adults," said John. "Two of them are kids."

Max shrugged. "They fight like adults. They have to survive just like everyone else."

"It's still different."

"We'll have to agree to disagree."

"So I'm thinking that..."

"You think we should run, right?" said Max, eyeing his brother's shifting eyes. Their eyes were what made them look the most similar. Max hadn't seen himself in a mirror in months, but he saw a part of himself in his brother's eyes.

John nodded. "Yeah," he said. "I know it's bad out there, but... I just don't see how we're going to get through this. Sooner or later we're going to have dozens of armed people invading again. And we're tired. We're not as well-fed or rested as we should be."

"We have the venison."

"But they could starve us out essentially. With the mob so close, it's going to be harder and harder to go out hunting. What if it takes weeks for them to attack? We'll just get weaker and weaker."

Max said nothing. He was deep in thought.

"Georgia's stronger than before, but she's not her old self. And no offense, but you and Mandy aren't looking so great yourselves."

"We're fine," said Max.

"So what do you think? You were out there. Down south. You think we should move on?"

"In what?" said Max. "The van?"

John nodded.

"We can't do it," said Max. "Even if we got the van running, our odds are going to be worse out there. Things haven't settled down. I don't know if they're getting worse or staying the same. It doesn't really matter. But we need to be out of whatever's going on."

"I thought everyone was dying off. The population numbers are going down."

Max nodded. "Yeah, but there's evidence of something else going on... people getting more organized."

"Like the militia, or what?"

"Something like that," said Max. He told John about a couple of the encounters he and Mandy had while out on the road. He told him about the people who'd been drugged up in the highway rest stop. He told him about the cowboy who hadn't seemed scared whatsoever.

"I don't see how that means anything," said John.

"Those are just minor encounters. It's not like an army or anything."

"You're not looking at it the right way. Those people being kept there," said Max. "It points to a group with a high level of organization. It points to a group that has the basics already covered, to the point where they can expend the energy and manpower going off to do whatever the hell it was they were doing."

"What in the world are you two chatting about?" called out Cynthia.

They both turned to look. Cynthia was striding over to them.

"You're probably sharing secret venison recipes, I bet."

John gave a little laugh.

Max remained stone-faced.

"My brother thinks we should get the hell out of here," said Max.

Cynthia's face fell.

"I thought you said we could make it," she said, glaring at John. "What? You keep your real thoughts to yourself and your brother? You don't want to tell the rest of us?"

"He thinks he's protecting you."

"Protecting us from what? How many times have our lives already been on the line?"

"I was just trying to..." said John.

But Cynthia didn't let him continue. "I can't believe it," she said, cutting him off.

"Don't take it the wrong way."

"I'll take it anyway I want to."

A gunshot rang out.

The three of them jumped into action.

Max reached for his Glock in its holster. He had it out in a flash. His rifle was back by the campfire.

"Everyone into position," shouted Georgia.

"Anyone hit?" shouted Cynthia.

John and Cynthia threw themselves behind nearby trees to give themselves places to shoot from, places where they'd have more shelter.

Those around the campfire were scattering. Max's eyes found Mandy. She was rushing off.

Max didn't jump for cover. Instead, he threw himself to the ground.

His eyes were scanning, looking for where the shot had come from.

It didn't seem like anyone had been hit.

Georgia finally had the man in her scope. She pulled the trigger.

The gun kicked.

A clean shot right to the heart.

Was that it?

Or were there more coming?

Max, Glock in hand, was dashing off into the woods, in the direction that the man had come from.

"Max!" John called out. "What are you doing?"

But Max didn't say anything. He didn't even turn around and look. He just dashed off, his gait a little lopsided from his injured leg.

It was a good thing he'd been shown where the ditch was.

Georgia was glad they'd gotten it finished. It now encircled the camp completely, and it was filled with sticks they'd carved into vicious points.

But would the ditch be enough?

Georgia didn't think so. It was shallow. And how many would fall in there before the rest realized what was up? It depended upon how "aware" the individual mob members were.

Georgia didn't think it'd be that effective.

But it'd be something.

"Everyone stay in position," called out Georgia.

She glanced back at Sadie and James, who were safely behind her, having taken cover behind some trees. They'd discussed what to do in this scenario.

Everyone was where they were supposed to be.

Except for Max.

Georgia hoped he knew what he was doing.

Normally he was cautious. Normally he did the right thing, acting and thinking strategically.

It wasn't like him to run off like that. Unless there was a good reason. A very good reason.

Georgia knew that the big attack was coming. But she didn't know when.

In her gut, it seemed like it couldn't be now. Not yet. Another week maybe, and the mob would be more restless, hungrier, more desperate.

Max was completely out of view.

But apparently not out of earshot.

Three popping sounds erupted. Sounded like Max's Glock.

Footsteps on the ground.

It was Max, running back. He leaped easily over the camouflaged ditch, ran straight to Georgia, and threw himself down next to her.

There was sweat on his face and his eyes were wide.

Georgia looked into his eyes, expecting to get reassurance. So often he was calm when the rest of them weren't.

But what she saw shocked her and made her heart start thumping.

His eyes were wild with fear. He looked frantic, like he was barely keeping it together.

"What is it?"

"They're coming."

Georgia waited.

They'd known that was a possibility. They'd known it would happen eventually.

There must have been something more.

"There's more of them than we thought," said Max.

"How many?"

"Maybe fifty."

"Fifty!"

Georgia felt her heart sink. She felt her gut tensing and tightening, as if it was bound together by iron.

Fifty! There was no way they could survive that.

"We can't beat fifty of them," said Georgia. "There's no way." She was talking fast and anxiously. And that was rare for her. "We've got to get out of here. Get the hell out of here."

"I think it's too late for that."

Georgia aimed her rifle towards the other side of the camp, using her scope to see far off into the distance.

There were people. Various states of dress and undress. Torn and tattered clothing. Some wore no clothing at all. Just what they were used to, just what the mob looked like.

Some of them were rail-thin. Some were more muscular. Most had long tangled hair.

Some were covered in blisters and cuts that oozed. Some were covered in scrapes. Some were covered in bandages.

Some carried weapons. Many of them guns.

There were at least a dozen coming from down the

road that Max and Mandy had only recently arrived on, the road that they'd left days ago on in the pickup.

"Maybe we can fight our way out that way," said Georgia. "Maybe we can..."

Max shook his head. "We've got to stay and stand our ground," he said. "There's no telling how many more there are in that direction. I don't like the situation either, but..."

Georgia said nothing for a couple seconds.

"I know you're right, but I don't want to admit it. You've got a weird ability of always being right about these things."

"Everyone!" shouted Max. "We've got fifty or more people coming."

"Fifty!" cried out Cynthia.

"Grab as many guns as you can. Rifles, handguns. Whatever. Get your knives. As much ammunition as you can carry. Now's the chance to get them. There isn't going to be another one."

"Mom?" cried out Sadie. "What's going to happen?"

Everyone was shouting out from their hiding places. It was a strange way to have a conversation.

"I don't know, Sadie," said Georgia. "Just do what Max says."

No one was moving. The news of fifty people had sent them into panic. Fear. Shock.

Max stood up.

"Come on, everyone," he shouted. "Get those weapons! Now! We're not going to have another chance."

Max was a flurry of action himself. He was at the van, grabbing the guns and distributing them.

Georgia got up, went over to Sadie, took her by the hand and led her to Max and the van.

"Two rifles, Sadie," said Georgia. "At the very least."

"Mom, I'm scared."

"'There's no time for that now, Sadie," said Georgia.

She was scared herself.

And it pained her to be telling her daughter to take more than one rifle. Sure, they'd been in bad situations before. But this was different.

This might very well be the end. She might see her daughter and son shot. She might get shot herself, or get bludgeoned to death with some blunt instrument right in front of her children.

It was too much. It was all too much.

But she had to press on. She had to fight.

Because there were no other options.

"How the hell could there possibly be fifty of them?" said Cynthia, her voice cutting through the clatter of guns and gear.

"Maybe it's the last of a group fleeing the cities," said John. "Who knows."

He was checking his handgun, two rifles slung already over his shoulder. His pockets were weighed down with ammunition. He'd taken another knife from somewhere.

"I just can't believe it," said Cynthia.

"We've got to believe it," said Max. "Because it's the only reality that we have."

"Maybe this'll be it," said Mandy. "Maybe this will be the final fight."

"You mean we're going to die?" said Cynthia. "Is that what you mean by final fight?"

"No. I mean that maybe if we can just get through this, once things finally calm down..."

"That's what we're always hoping for and it never happens."

"Enough chatting," said Max, his voice cutting through, sounding harsh. But he was right. There was too much to do.

"You three," said Georgia. "We're taking the north side." She'd pointed to John and Cynthia. She couldn't bear the thought of having her children at her side. If they were out of sight, she knew she could fight better without worrying about them. In a way, it was almost worse not having her eyes on them. But she couldn't deal with the distraction.

"We can't hold off fifty with just us."

"We'll see how it goes," said Max. "It's not like we have a lot of room to work with anyway. We're going to have to play this one by ear. There's no outsmarting a mob. No outmaneuvering them. Just fighting."

"You sure this is the way?" said Rob as the car trundled down an unpaved road through a thickly wooded area.

"Nope," said Dan. "I'm not."

"But this is your best guess, right?"

"Exactly."

They'd driven for a day straight, somehow avoiding any trouble on the road. The old car had threatened to give up the ghost more than once, but somehow it had kept going. Rob had had to drive slower after a while, because the engine had started making loud noises at any speed above sixty. Some kind of strange whirring noise, as if a belt was about to fly completely off.

They'd found a plastic gas can in the trunk, which they'd used to partially refill the tank.

They drove for another half hour without seeing anything.

"The sign said it was the hunting grounds, or whatever it's called," said Olivia. "This must be the place."

"Let's just hope there's someone still here," said Rob. "And that they're friendly. You trust this guy? What was his name, again?"

"Max," said Dan. "Yeah, I mean as much as you can trust someone you've met over the radio."

"I don't see what the point would be of luring someone so far down to a camp in the middle of the woods," said Olivia. "I mean, what would be the point?"

"Stranger things have happened," said Rob. "But we're ready for whatever happens." He patted his handgun's holster. "I'd just rather that it didn't go down like that."

"I mean before the EMP, sure, I'd be suspicious of going to meet some guy in the woods that you met on the radio," said Olivia. "But now..."

"Basically, if you were a serial killer or something now, there'd be plenty of targets all over," said Rob. "No need to lure anyone. Is that what you're saying?"

"I guess so. But that's not very positive."

"Who said anything about being positive?"

"Look!" said Dan, pointing out the window. He was sitting in the front seat now.

Up ahead, there were a couple people in the middle of the dirt road. Their clothes were tattered and one of them was so thin that Dan couldn't believe she was still standing on her own two feet.

They staggered more than they walked, shuffling forward aimlessly.

"Now's the time to make a joke about zombie movies," said Rob.

Neither Olivia or Dan responded.

"Really? Nothing? That's the best I've got tonight. Tough crowd."

"Since when did you start treating this all like a standup comedy routine?"

"It happens sometimes when I get really tired. I didn't see either of you offering to drive."

"What are we going to do?" said Dan.

"You think there's any chance that's your friend Max? Because if it is, I don't think he's going to be much help to us."

"No," said Dan. "There's no way."

But inside, he wasn't sure. Max had sounded so intelligent and competent over the radio. For the first time, a new possibility hit him. The possibility that Max and his friends were alive, that Dan had found them, but that they themselves were in terrible shape, just barely hanging on, and about to starve to death.

"Well," said Rob. "I've got one idea. These people don't look like much of a threat. But get ready for a fight, even so."

Dan already had his handgun in hand.

Rob honked the horn. It was an ancient horn, but it still worked.

The people in the road turned back vaguely to look.

Rob kept driving. He was driving slowly at this point, mostly because of the bumps in the road.

The strangers in the road finally parted, standing to the side, and staring blankly at the car as it drove past.

"Let's hope there aren't a lot of people like that around," said Rob. "They can be a big problem."

"They don't seem like much of a threat," said Olivia.

"You wouldn't think so, yeah. But I've seen them go nuts. It doesn't take much. Sometimes a gunshot. Sometimes something else."

"Like what?"

"A glimpse of food. A glimpse of a better life."

"What do you mean by they go nuts?"

"There's no better way to say it. They go insane. They've already lost everything that makes them human. Or maybe they're just becoming more human than ever. Most animalistic. There's no way to know. Anyway, this isn't the time for a philosophical discussion like that..."

They continued driving slowly down the road.

"Do you hear that?" said Olivia.

"Yeah, sounds like gunshots," said Dan.

"I don't hear them," said Rob. A moment later he said, "Oh, yeah."

They were getting more frequent. And they were getting louder the farther along the road they went.

"What should we do?" said Olivia, sounding nervous. "Do you think we should turn around?"

"I think it's too late for that," said Rob, glancing into the rearview mirror. "Take a look behind us."

There were dozens of people on the road behind them. Dan turned around fully to get a better look. He couldn't see their eyes very clearly, but he could see the expressions on their faces. And they showed him nothing but rage and anger. Nothing but violence.

"Can't you just drive through them?" said Olivia, sounding more frantic with each word she spoke.

"No," said Rob, shaking his head. "We'll never get through all of them."

"What are we going to do, then?" Olivia's voice had gotten high with worry.

Dan's heart was pounding and his hands felt shaky as he watched the mob behind them. Slowly, they were advancing, closing the gap between themselves and the slow-moving car.

"We've got to keep going forward."

"What if there are more of them?"

"Let's hope there's someone at this camp that can help us."

25

MAX

Max had a man in his sights. He didn't hesitate. There wasn't any time.

He pulled the trigger. The rifle kicked.

The man fell.

A good clean shot. Right to the heart.

But they were still coming. Seemingly from all sides.

"There are too many of them," shouted John.

"Shut up and keep shooting," shouted Cynthia right back at him.

Time seemed to have slowed down. Every second seemed to stretch into an eternity.

The landscape seemed to have changed along with the distortion in time. The colors of the trees and the ground, of the tent and the van, they all seemed more vibrant than ever.

Max knew it was just the adrenaline. The thrill of the fight, in a sense.

His body was doing everything it could to keep him alive.

The sounds of the guns seemed continuous. It had

dulled to a roar that seemed just like part of the background, as if it had always been there.

John had abandoned his rifle for one of the guns he and Cynthia had brought along. Some kind of AK-47 knockoff. Even cheaper and cruder than the original, but it seemed to do the job.

John's face was contorted in intensity and rage. His mouth had formed into a snarl.

John looked completely different than he had as a kid. Or even as an adult, before the EMP. He'd been clean-cut. He'd had good clothes.

Now, his beard was getting long and his hair was unruly. There was dirt and grime on his face. He'd grown gaunter. Leaner. And more muscular.

He looked like a different man altogether.

Cynthia was sorting through the guns and ammunition, handing out weapons to everyone in the group.

The initial split of the group, with some of them going in one direction, and others in another, had lasted all of ten minutes. They'd quickly had to fall back into a small group, huddled around the van.

Not many of the mob members seemed to have guns. But that didn't mean they weren't dangerous.

Max's group was mowing them down now, shooting them at a distance.

But with each passing minute, the mob, which was coming from all sides, was getting closer. Individuals were starting to break through the invisible line that separated them from the group.

A wild-looking man was rushing at them. He was sprinting right towards Max.

He was ten feet away.

Now five.

Max could see his face and eyes clearly. He could see the rage and the contempt, and the savageness that had broken through to the surface, that had taken him over completely.

A gunshot rang out. One that Max heard clearly, distinct from the others.

A spot of blood appeared on the wild man's forehead. He seemed to remain upright for far too long before collapsing, almost right at Max's feet.

"They're getting closer!" someone shouted.

A group of two or three people had broken through the line of carnage.

They leaped over the bodies of their fallen comrades, if you could call them that. They sprinted towards Max's group.

Max tossed his rifle aside and Cynthia handed him something else. He barely looked at it.

It was a semi-automatic. He opened fire, pulling the trigger in rapid succession. He hit one of them, a woman with long hair that streamed behind her. But the shot didn't take her down. She kept running, her face a mixture of pain and anger.

"Behind you!" shouted Georgia.

Max spun around.

A dozen or so had broken through.

Everyone was shooting. Even Sadie, who was fighting with determination, not breaking into panic.

Mandy was at Max's side. Close. Her elbow knocked into him occasionally. Her hair had come undone. Her forehead was beaded with sweat. But she'd never looked more beautiful.

This might be the last time he saw her alive. The

thought ran through Max's mind like an icepick, piercing him, causing him pain.

James was on the ground on his belly, his rifle positioned perfectly, just like his mother had taught him. He remained calm and worked like a flawless machine. He took aim, pulled the trigger, did it again. He reloaded like it was second nature, like the gun was part of him.

They were all doing their best. They'd learned a lot. All of them. Max included.

But it wasn't enough.

John was firing in the opposite direction. Mandy was pointed that way too.

Max had taken three of the breakthrough group out. Their bodies lay forgotten on the campground. But the rest were closing in fast.

They were close. Too close.

One wielded an axe. Another, a saw.

One had a metal baseball bat.

Another, nothing more than a piece of dead wood, probably picked up from the forest floor.

But it didn't matter. If they got close enough, if they broke through, they could cause enough damage with whatever blunt or sharp instrument they had.

The mob didn't care about dying. They were too filled with rage and desperation to think about their own mortality. It simply didn't matter to them. They were like insects, protecting their hive, ready to die. Except that the mob had no hive and nothing to protect. In that way, they were more dangerous.

Max's group was barely holding it off as it was. If Max got hit in the head with a baseball bat, the group's effectiveness would plummet. Even if he could shake it off, that one brief moment would be enough to start their down-fall snowballing.

It'd be those little moments, those small injuries, that would bring them down.

As he was firing, Max's thoughts drifted to the members of his group. He couldn't help himself. It felt as if he was looking at them for the last time. Their faces seemed frozen in time. Maybe that'd be the last time they'd be seen by anyone before they became dismembered corpses. Probably eaten raw later on by men and women who had become barely human, or maybe all too human, depending on how you looked at it.

Max wanted to do something. He'd sacrifice himself if it would do any good.

He'd be willing to run head-first into the mob, guns blazing, if it would have made the slightest difference.

But there was nothing he could do. There was no grand gesture. No last minute play.

And they were surrounded. Max couldn't have broken free if he'd wanted to. Not that sneaking around the side would have done any good.

No strategy would save them.

Through the gunshots, Max heard another noise. It came through the roaring of the mob, somehow cutting through.

It was a machine. An engine.

His brain struggled to attach meaning to the noise. He felt scrambled. Like he couldn't think.

His finger had been pumping the trigger. The gun was hot.

The smell of death was in the air.

Blood was everywhere.

Some of the men and women had made it all the way there.

Max shot one of them in the chest at close range. Nearly point blank.

Someone behind him turned around and fired. Georgia or John. He wasn't sure.

It was happening so fast, despite the adrenaline-fueled slow motion.

Something slammed into his head. Something hard. His vision shook for a second, the world seemingly tilting on its axis.

The gun was pulled from Max's hands. No matter how hard he gripped, it wasn't enough. There were four or five or six hands on the gun.

Something slammed into Max's shoulder.

A fist slammed into his stomach, knocking the breath out of him.

He gasped for air. His head felt like it was on fire.

They were all around him.

Max's hand went for his knife. Somehow, he found it.

He gripped it tightly and brought his hand up swiftly, swinging with his arm viciously.

He caught someone in the neck. A long, slicing cut. But deep.

Hot blood was all over. Max tasted it in his mouth. He felt it on his face.

That strange sound of the engine was coming back, rising above the din of the battle at hand.

Yes, it was an engine. Max's mind focused in on it, like a camera lens.

The engine roared. It was close now.

Max looked up. He was on his knees, with a body lying on the ground in front of him.

Somehow, those who'd broken through had been killed.

But those were just the first.

More were coming. At least another dozen.

The roar of the engine was closer. Coming from the south side, where Max faced.

Max saw the flash of a chrome bumper first.

It was a car. His exhausted brain registered on it and categorized it.

A car that was speeding through the rushing mob. It was something like an old Chrysler, decades out of date. It jumped and careened over the uneven terrain, mowing down countless mob members as it did.

The car left a tangle of bodies in its wake. It bounced over some of them. One careened off the bumper and landed on the windshield, cracking it.

Some of the mob had jumped out of the way successfully. Max didn't waste any time. He seized his gun from where it lay in the dirt. He caught them in his sights and pulled the trigger in rapid succession.

The car kept coming. Someone, alive or dead, lay on the windshield.

It went right over the shallow ditch, the car barely buckling as it did so. So much for that plan with the ditch. It hadn't stopped more than a couple of the mob members. It might have turned an ankle or two, and some of the spikes might have torn someone's skin, but that was about it.

Could the driver even see out?

The car slammed to a stop mere feet from Max.

The door flew open.

A large man stepped out, holding what looked like an AR-15.

"Max?" he said, flashing a lopsided grin that looked more like a grimace than anything else.

Max didn't know who the man was, or how he knew his name. But there wasn't time to get into it. As far as he could tell, the man was on his side.

Max just nodded.

Inside the car, there was a woman and a teenage boy.

The kid, holding a handgun, was already halfway out the back door.

The mob was still coming. The car hadn't stopped nearly enough of them.

But it had made an impact.

All around them, the fighting continued.

"More coming from the north," shouted Georgia, over the gunshots that never seemed to stop.

But before Max could even turn, there was another rush from the mob coming from the south.

They screamed as they ran. Max tried to keep it together as much as he could, knowing that his aim would be better. He focused on his breathing, and taking the time to aim properly.

Shooting at random wouldn't accomplish anything. And at this point, every bullet needed to count.

The car would serve as a sort of barrier. The big man with the AR-15 was already crouching down behind the hood, shooting over it.

The kid with the handgun was unloading it into the crowd.

"Help!" shouted someone.

"Help!"

Max couldn't turn. If he looked away for a moment, they'd be overrun. They'd just have to hold out as best they could on the other side.

They were coming in from all sides. At each moment, it seemed like they'd be overrun.

John expected he'd die at any moment. He was OK with that. It was what it was. He knew that Max felt the same way.

But he wasn't going to let his life go in vain.

If there was just the slimmest chance that he could help save his friends, or some of them, he'd do anything.

But that was where the frustration came in.

There wasn't anything to do. There wasn't any way, as far as he could see, to sacrifice himself for the benefit of his friends.

Cynthia was next to him. Close by. She'd ceased making sarcastic remarks. That was one barometer for how serious the situation was.

"I'm out of ammo!" shouted Cynthia, above the roar of the mob, the screams of pain and the shouts of anger.

With one hand, John fished into his pocket and grabbed a clip. He couldn't take his eyes off the mob. He held his hand out and felt Cynthia grab it.

Something had happened behind him. Some kind of vehicle. It didn't seem to be a threat, so John didn't bother shifting his attention.

Suddenly, something slammed into his shoulder.

It took him a moment to realize what had happened.

It was a bullet.

Not far away, a woman in her fifties held a handgun in an outstretched arm.

A moment later, bullets ripped into her chest, and she collapsed face-first into the dirt.

Everything was collapsing. The mob was gaining ground.

From the east, someone had broken through, reaching the van where the group was.

John saw the flurry of movement more than he saw the person. It was a man. Someone big. That was all he registered.

John needed to keep shooting to keep the mob at bay.

But someone needed to deal with this man who'd broken through.

The man brandished a tire iron. He was headed right for James, who hadn't even taken his eyes off his scope.

John would have to be the one to act. The others could keep shooting.

The tire iron man was caught up in the midst of John's friends. John couldn't get a good clean shot. It'd have to be hand-to-hand. Or something like it.

John moved as fast as he could. His body was in pain, sore and exhausted. But he was also pumped full of adrenaline.

The man with the tire iron saw him moving, seemed to sense the threat. He stopped where he was, the tire iron raised.

This wasn't the time for subtlety.

John rushed him, swinging the gun in his right hand in a wide arc.

The tire iron collided with it, knocked it out of John's hand. It clattered to the dirt.

John went for his knife in its holster.

But it was too late.

The tire iron collided with his shoulder, sending pain shooting through him. His arm felt immobilized. It hung limply at his side.

The tire iron was swinging again.

John raised his left hand swiftly. He caught the iron. It slammed into his palm but he ignored the pain and wrapped his fingers around it.

He pulled the tire iron toward himself swiftly and with as much force as he could.

This pulled the man towards him.

John brought up his knee. He caught the man in the stomach. Hard.

He heard the breath escape him.

John tugged on the tire iron. But the other man's grip was strong. He couldn't get it free.

John brought his knee up again. He still couldn't move his right arm much, but he was starting to feel twinges of feeling in his hand where it had gone numb.

Someone else was near him. A flash of movement. A long coat swirling with movement. John only got impressions of what was happening.

John's mind tried to move his right arm up to defend himself. Desperately. But the arm didn't move.

John's knee slammed again into the man's stomach. He was still pulling on the tire iron as hard as he could.

Something slammed into his head from the right. Felt like a rock. Maybe it was just a fist.

Gunshots all around him.

Someone else had broken past the line, gotten into the little huddle of desperate survivors by the van.

John was out of options.

He threw his head forward as hard as he could, going for a head-butt. Just like he used to do in soccer when he was a kid.

His forehead slammed into the man's face. Blood was everywhere. On John's face, too.

Something slammed into his head again. His vision went blurry.

A gun sounded right next to his ear.

He went almost deaf. Nothing but ringing in his ears.

Pain in his right arm now. Something was grabbing it.

The man in the coat to his right had fallen. His head had broken open like a watermelon. The upper portion of his skull had exploded into fragments. Almost like a busted watermelon lying on the ground. His brain was exposed, the wrinkled substance looking strange there on the ground.

The brain was some of the most advanced biology in the world, and it was lying there useless on the ground. Destroyed. And what had it accomplished before its end? Nothing. It hadn't been able to keep up. It hadn't been able to adapt.

The long coat lay spread out on the ground like an angel's wings.

John's brain was going to weird places. It was exhausted. It was stressed. It was losing track of what was happening.

Everything seemed to be happening both slowly and quickly.

John felt something crash into his face. The man with the tire iron had head-butted him. John tasted his own blood now. His nose was probably broken.

Another rapid burst of gunfire. Close enough that John could hear it over the intense ringing in his ears.

The neck and head of the man in front of him were suddenly ripped to shreds. Blood covered John.

The man's face fell apart. Exposed bone. Cartilage. Huge chunks of flesh just hanging there. A bullet lodged into his eye.

Even in death, he gripped the tire iron tightly.

John finally let go.

He reached for his handgun with his good left hand, but it wasn't in its holster.

He couldn't remember what had happened to it.

The fog had entered his mind.

He was confused. Deaf. Disoriented.

His head turned rapidly as he took in the landscape.

All he saw, out past the van, were bodies. Bodies rushing at them. Bodies screaming, in pain and anger and violence. Bodies falling. Bodies lying dead on the ground. Bodies with various injuries.

This was what the world had come to.

Rob didn't know who he was fighting with. But he knew what he was fighting for.

Survival.

And he knew who he was fighting. He was fighting violence and evil. He was fighting the worst of humanity. When there was nothing left, when there was nothing left to hem it all in, the violence and anger exploded out of the individuals. They'd become something else entirely.

What was he doing here?

It didn't seem like they'd make it.

It wasn't the safe haven he'd thought it'd be.

He'd seen the signs coming in. He'd seen the people walking like stragglers, lumbering along with that blank look in their eyes.

He must have known, somewhere deep inside himself, that he wasn't going to find safety.

He could have turned around.

Hell, he could have left the kid and Olivia there on their own. He'd already helped them once. He didn't owe them anything.

Maybe it'd been the memory of his own family that'd pushed him to do it. He'd wanted to get the kid to a safe place, even if he'd never admit that out loud.

The memories of his wife and son and daughter were still fresh in his mind. He could laugh all he want. He could chuckle and act like nothing was a big deal. But that didn't mean that he didn't see their faces each time he closed his eyes. It didn't mean that he didn't feel the terrible pain in his heart when he thought of them and their deaths.

The sound of the battle raged around him.

Rob was taking them out. He was shooting methodically. He was working like a machine. He was barely pausing to breathe.

His heart was pounding. He was covered in sweat.

There was a young girl running around handing out ammunition to everyone. She carried it in huge duffel bags. She had to sort through it to find what was needed.

She was there now, handing the kid Dan a couple clips for his handgun.

"You got any for me?" shouted Rob.

She glanced into her bag. She wore two rifles strapped to her back. They looked far too big for her.

But she knew how to use them. He'd seen her shoot a woman in the head without flinching. Without batting an eyelash.

"Here," she said, shoving some clips into the pocket of his light jacket.

Rob nodded at her and she scurried off behind him out of view.

Rob slammed the clips into his AR-15.

Three men were coming for them at an angle. They were young. Somewhere in their twenties.

It was a shame.

They could have been something. They could have done something with their lives.

But the EMP had changed everything.

Rob pulled the trigger. He caught one in the chest. He fell. Didn't scream. Didn't cry out. Just fell face-down into the dirt.

His companions did nothing. They didn't even seem to notice.

They were too far gone for that.

Olivia, who was stuck in the car, was shooting out the window with a handgun. It seemed that she barely knew how to use it. But she was trying. Once in a while, she'd hit someone.

Rob wondered if he should tell the girl, next time she came around, if she should give Olivia any more ammunition or not. He didn't know how much ammo was left. And he didn't know if Olivia was using it wisely or not.

But there probably wouldn't be any choice either way.

The mob couldn't be held off much longer.

Twenty of them were rushing.

And it didn't seem to be the last of them.

Gunshots sang out around him.

Rob's ears were ringing intensely.

He took aim. Pulled the trigger. Got one in the arm. Pulled the trigger again. Hit the chest this time.

A couple more fell. But there were too many.

Many of Rob's new companions were facing other directions. The mob was on all sides.

There wasn't enough firepower aimed at the rushing mob.

Rob couldn't take them all out himself.

Olivia didn't know what she was doing.

And the kid wasn't a whole hell of a lot better.

It was up to Rob.

He glanced at the kid. There was something about him that reminded him of his own son. He didn't know what it was. After all, his own son had only been four years old. But there was something about the attitude, the diligence and determination that was spread across Dan's face.

Rob knew what he had to do.

The door to the car was already open. He reached in, grabbed Olivia roughly by the arm, and yanked her towards him.

"What are you doing?" she cried out.

Rob could barely hear her. Her cry sounded faint and distant.

She fought against him.

But Rob was stronger. Her pulled harder.

He let his AR-15 drop out of his hands. It hung behind him at his side on its sling.

He grabbed her with both hands and pulled her completely out of the car.

"What!" she screamed at him.

Her face looked up at him. He saw the betrayal that she felt.

But there wasn't any time to explain.

He had to act fast.

"What are you doing, Rob? Rob!" it was the kid, shouting at him.

"I'm going in. Don't hold back your fire!"

"What? What the hell are you talking about?"

They could barely hear each other.

"Don't hold your fire!" shouted Rob again. "Don't hold

your fire!" He needed the message to get through. No matter what. He needed Dan to understand.

Olivia lay on the ground at Rob's feet. She was in pain. It was all over her face. He'd probably hurt her injury by yanking her out of the car like that, dumping her on the ground. But he was doing it to save her life.

Rob stepped over her and slid into the passenger's seat.

The keys were still in the ignition.

The car was still running.

He glanced at the gas gauge.

It was on empty.

But he didn't have to drive far.

"What are you doing?" screamed Dan.

Rob knew what he was doing. And there wasn't time to respond.

He threw the car into reverse and hit the accelerator.

He jammed his boot to the floor. The engine roared. But he barely even heard it over the ringing in his ears.

The wheels spun in the dirt.

Would the car move or was it stuck?

The wheels kept spinning.

Finally, something happened. He felt the jolt as the tires dug out of the rut.

The car rocketed backwards.

That was good. He hadn't been sure it was going to make it. It had taken a lot of damage from the people he'd run over.

Rob had one hand on the wheel, his other arm extended. His whole body was turned and he looked out the back windshield, which wasn't yet shattered.

The car was rear wheel drive. But he didn't have to turn it much.

He headed in a straight line right for the rushing mob.

He hit the first one.

A sickening thud.

If there was a scream, he didn't hear it.

The gunshots around him didn't let up.

Rob's boot didn't budge from the accelerator.

He knew he was going down. He knew this was his last drive. He knew these were his last moments.

He just hoped that Dan would keep shooting as he'd ordered.

Rob had to take out as many of them as he could if the kid and the others were going to have a chance.

It didn't seem strange to sacrifice himself for people he barely knew. It didn't feel good either. It didn't really feel like anything at all.

The only feeling Rob had was that he had a purpose. He had a goal. He was going to make it work.

He let his eyes close for a brief moment as the car careened backwards. He saw his family there.

A thud.

Another one down.

Rob opened his eyes.

There were some of the mob members off to his right.

Rob yanked the wheel hard.

The car swerved.

He hit them with the side of the car.

Then another impact.

The car shuddered.

The back wheels spun uselessly.

The car was tilted slightly.

The wheels were stuck in some kind of rut. Or a ditch.

There were people all around him. They crowded the car. He saw the violence on their faces.

They'd surrounded the car.

Good. He'd distracted them.

Now all the kid and Max and the others had to do was keep shooting. They just needed to realize that Rob was a lost cause, and not to worry that they'd hit him with friendly fire.

Rob couldn't tell if they were shooting or not. There wasn't any point in worrying about it.

Two strong hands reached in at him through the passenger's side window. The window was down.

Rob pulled on the sling of his gun, got it into position. His hands gripped it.

It wasn't a bad way to go out. Gun in hand. Fighting the good fight. There were worse things that could have happened.

His finger was working the trigger.

The gun recoiled in his hands.

Someone was yanking the driver's side door open. Rob hadn't had time to lock it. Wouldn't have mattered, anyway.

Rob picked up his feet and spun his body around on the battered upholstery.

He was facing the open driver's side door. He kicked with both feet. One boot collided with someone's stomach. The other slammed into the door. Pain shot through him.

He got his gun facing the right way. He pulled the trigger.

Someone screamed.

Blood.

Someone fell.

Someone grabbed the gun. Gaunt thin hands that shouldn't have been as strong as they were.

Four hands on the gun. Now six.

He couldn't hold onto it.

He pulled the trigger one last time. A bullet went somewhere. He wasn't sure where.

The gun was yanked from him. His hands hurt from trying to hold onto it.

He saw the gun go out of view. Any second, he was expecting it to be turned on him.

But the mob wasn't thinking. Through the crowd of hands and bodies in front of him, he glimpsed the gun one last time as it fell, unused, to the ground.

Hands were on him. They were trying to pull him from the car.

Rob grabbed his handgun. The safety was off.

He took aim at the nearest head. He pulled the trigger. The gun kicked and the man fell, most of his face missing.

Before Rob could pull the trigger again, hands were on the handgun.

He pulled the trigger anyway.

A scream.

A bullet had pierced someone's hand. Maybe two hands.

But the gun was ripped away from him.

Rob kicked out with his boot as hard as he could.

But hands caught him around the ankle and pulled him from the car.

Rob's head slammed against the car as he fell.

He was on his back in the dirt.

They were all around him. Too many to count.

It was the end. But at least he'd taken a lot of them out.

But it wasn't quite the end.

Rob reached for his knife. A large, combat style knife. Sharpened on both sides. Made of good steel.

Boots and shoes and bare feet collided with his stomach. They were kicking him all over. On his back. His shoulder. His feet.

A piece of wood swung like a club and smashed into his skull.

His vision went funny.

Knife in hand, Rob swung his arm. The knife slashed against an ankle. Someone screamed.

Why weren't they shooting?

Rob would have preferred going out by friendly fire if it meant that he'd done something. The whole point was to distract them enough that the kid and the others could take them out one by one. But it seemed like they were delaying for the sake of Rob.

But Rob knew he was gone anyway.

And then it happened.

He didn't hear the gunshot. There was too much gunfire. Too much chaos and too much noise.

He didn't see the bullet slam into the torso. But he saw the result. He saw the woman falling, and he saw the bullet wound.

They were shooting.

What he'd done had mattered. He accomplished what he'd set out to do.

Another one fell. Another bullet wound.

Something slammed into his head again.

His vision went black.

28

"**M**ax!"
But it was too late.
He wasn't stopping.

"Max! Stop!" called out Mandy, as loud as she could. Her voice sounded frantic and she didn't care.

Max was sprinting towards the car. Sprinting towards the group that had surrounded Rob.

Mandy hadn't seen it until it was too late. She'd been busy with the other side.

When she'd finally turned, Max had already been running across the dirt. He carried only his Glock. His coat and pants were torn. His gait was uneven because of his leg.

She couldn't see his face. But she knew what expression she would have seen.

Mandy didn't know who the man in the car was. And neither did Max.

But he was still risking his life for him.

Mandy trained her rifle on one of the men who was beating the stranger on the ground. It looked like they were about to kill him. Or maybe they already had.

Mandy could make it easier for Max.

She pulled the trigger.

But nothing happened. It seemed like it was jammed.

Mandy's brain was a mess. She couldn't remember what she was supposed to do. She slammed her fist into the rifle in frustration and tossed it to the side.

All around her, her friends were still fighting.

The mob had been thinned considerably. They'd almost made it. But those who were left were still coming.

Georgia was picking them off one by one with machine-like precision and control.

John and Cynthia had ventured into the fray, into the scattered mob. They were shooting them at closer range.

Some of the mob were lying on the ground, half alive. Some had given up, and were simply sitting in place.

Others were still fighting, still rushing the van.

The mob was a broken mess. Disorganized and destroyed.

But still dangerous.

Max, off in the opposite direction of Cynthia and John, was firing as he ran. His Glock was held outstretched in front of him.

Mandy grabbed her own handgun and dashed off towards Max.

A hand reached out for her. It was a man in his twenties, wearing no shirt and nothing but tattered underwear. He held a meat cleaver in his other hand.

The cleaver swung towards Mandy.

She shot him with her handgun. It was almost all automatic. She barely had to think about it.

She took aim and pulled the trigger and the young

man fell, his cleaver falling with him in his clenched fist to the ground.

Mandy sprinted away from the body, towards Max.

Someone was running behind her. She checked over her shoulder. It was a kid with a gun in his hand. He wasn't part of the mob.

She ran on.

She didn't fire as she ran. She didn't want to hit Max.

She heard the Glock discharging.

She reached Max as he was plunging his knife into someone's stomach.

There was someone coming for Max, two hands on a stone that swung towards his head.

Mandy raised her gun, took aim at the woman's head, and pulled the trigger.

The bullet struck the woman in the arm. She didn't collapse, but the rock smashed into the ground rather than Max's head.

Max spun and, without hesitation, plunged his knife right into the woman's stomach.

The kid reached them, panting and out of breath, his gun raised.

The man who'd driven the car lay on the ground, bleeding from his head.

Mandy looked around. The mob was scattered. Most of them lay on the ground. Many of them were dead. The rest were injured, moaning and screaming and crying.

Mandy's ears were ringing. She was partially deaf.

The kid got down on the ground, dropping his gun into the dirt. He got both his hands on the stranger and started shaking him, as if he was trying to revive him. He was saying something, but Mandy couldn't hear what it was.

Max put his hands on the crying kid and pulled him away.

Mandy saw him open his mouth, but she heard nothing.

As Mandy looked around, her heart sank.

They were alive. Mandy and Max. John and Cynthia. James and Sadie.

But she didn't feel joy or triumph.

Her body was so weak she felt like she might collapse to the ground at any moment.

The carnage around them was horrible. Terrifying. And completely real. She could close her eyes, but it would never go away.

This was the world she lived in now.

29

MAX

Max woke up with a headache. His leg hurt and his entire body was sore from yesterday. He'd pushed it harder than he had in who knew how long. Maybe ever.

But he was alive. They were all alive. Except for Rob, who Max had barely met.

"You awake?" said Mandy, who lay beside him.

Max nodded.

"How'd you sleep?"

"Not good," said Max.

He didn't elaborate, but his dreams had been filled with nightmarish images of the carnage from yesterday.

"Me neither," said Mandy.

Max closed his eyes again, remembering yesterday.

It had seemed more like a series of days than a single day. The reality was, he didn't know how long it had all taken. His automatic watch, which had proven so durable on countless misadventures, had finally broken. The acrylic crystal hadn't cracked, and there were no marks on the stainless steel case, but the watch had finally stopped ticking. No matter how much he shook it or wound it, the red seconds hand didn't move.

The battle hadn't felt like it had really ever ended. There'd been no final victory to celebrate. There'd been no decisive moment that they had all seen.

Sure, Rob, whose name Max had finally learned, had helped turn the tide of the rushing mob. But the battle had continued after that.

The battle had simply continued to wind down, further and further.

Max and the others had split up into groups of two. They'd wandered the battlefield, walking between the corpses and the injured. For those that weren't yet completely dead, but lay bleeding out onto the dirt, Max and the others had shot them in the head. Usually point-blank range.

The images were still in Max's head. He'd shot more than the others. Mandy could barely stomach it. She'd shot one woman in the head, whose arm had almost been torn off, and then she'd thrown up. Mandy had been able to keep it together in the battle, but then the horror of the whole thing had come crashing down on her like a tidal wave.

The adrenaline of the battle had gradually worn off and they'd all been left exhausted, with the task of finishing the mob off.

It didn't seem like many of the mob had gotten away. When things had gotten bad, they'd started attacking each other.

Max remembered finding two men fighting each other. They'd been slashing at each other with axes, anger and rage on their faces. By the time Max had gotten to them, they were on the ground, both of them bleeding. They'd been lying on their backs, too injured to get back on their feet. They'd both been dying, bleeding rapidly out onto the dirt. But they'd still been slashing at each other, picking their arms up and letting them fall with the weight of the axe in their hand, hoping to strike one final blow.

It had been senseless. Senseless violence just for the sake of expressing frustration and anger.

Max had shot each in the head with his Glock. He'd done it calmly, his face impassive. He'd felt nothing when he'd done it. Nothing at all.

Now, the next day, he wasn't sure what he felt. He was pretty sure it was still nothing. Except for the headache and the bodily pain.

They'd fallen asleep outside, and the ground was cold.

Max opened his eyes again and sat up.

Bodies were everywhere. It'd been all they could do to put the injured ones out of their misery.

Today was cleanup day, taking the bodies off somewhere else. Or else move camp. And they weren't going to do that.

John and Dan were out there, walking together between the bodies. It looked like they were talking, but they were too far away to overhear.

Mandy sat up beside Max.

"What are you thinking about?" she said.

Her hair was a mess. It was tangled and a clump of it had been torn away. Her face was dirty and sweaty.

But to Max, she'd never looked better.

"I can't believe we're alive," he said.

Mandy flashed him a little smile with just the corners of her mouth.

Max leaned towards her and she leaned in towards him.

Their lips touched and they held them there for a moment, not moving them.

"Max," called out someone. "Max!"

Mandy pulled away from Max and pushed a strand of hair behind her ear.

Max looked up.

It was Dan, the kid who'd arrived yesterday, the one that he and Mandy had set out for.

He was walking towards Max with a serious expression on his face and his hand outstretched.

Max took it and Dan shook it vigorously.

"I know we met yesterday, but I just wanted to... introduce myself again."

Max nodded. "Yeah," he said. "Yesterday was intense. How you holding up?"

"Fine," said Dan. He had an eagerness on his face that hadn't been totally wiped out by yesterday, by the carnage, by the death of his friend.

"Sorry again about your friend," said Max, referring to Rob. "He did a hell of a thing."

Dan nodded. "The truth is, I barely knew him."

Max didn't say anything for a moment.

"We were trying to get to you," he said. "Me and Mandy here. We almost made it."

Dan nodded.

"Well," said Dan. "I don't want to bother you too much before your coffee. I'd better get back to work."

"What are you up to?"

"John and I are talking about what to do with the bodies."

"Not much to it," said Max. "We've got to just drag them away."

"Exactly. But I had an idea for a sort of sledge made out of wood. John's going to help me with it. Should cut down on the labor involved."

"Good idea," said Max. "See if you can find James around here. He might still be sleeping, but he can help you. We'll join you soon."

"How's your friend?" said Mandy. "The woman in the car?"

"She's OK," said Dan. "Her ankle's still hurting. She won't be able to help much today."

"I'm just glad she's still alive."

Off in the distance, John was calling out for Dan.

"Well, see you soon," said Dan, turning and jogging off towards John.

"He's got a lot of energy," said Mandy, watching him run off.

"More than that," said Max. "He's got the right attitude."

"How can you tell?"

"I can just tell."

"Well," said Mandy. "Let's get some coffee. Seems like we have a lot of work to do."

Max nodded, looking out again at all the bodies.

He stood up suddenly, brushing some of the dirt off his pants and shirt. His clothes were filthy and blood-stained.

He offered his hand to Mandy and he helped her to her feet.

Not far off, Georgia, James, Sadie, and Cynthia were getting ready for the day. They looked just as battered as Mandy and Max. But they were alive.

Georgia was giving orders to her kids, telling them to start getting breakfast ready. There was some food that Rob, Olivia, and Dan had brought down in the car with them. It would feed the group until they could hunt or trap some more deer.

Georgia saw Max looking off in their direction, and she gave him a nod before moving off to some chore or another. She liked to keep busy.

"Let's take a walk," said Max, looking Mandy in the eye.

"A walk? That doesn't sound like you."

"Not far," said Max. "I just want to get away from this for a moment."

"There's work to be done," said Mandy, gesturing out to the mounds of dead bodies that needed to be moved. "You're always like Georgia, telling us to get to work. More work to do. More, more, more." She smiled slightly at Max as she spoke, and he knew she was teasing him just a little.

Max tried to crack a smile but he couldn't quite do it. Not with what had happened. Not with the bodies everywhere.

"They're not going to miss us for a few minutes," said Max. "Come on, just a short walk."

"Really doesn't sound like you," muttered Mandy, but she followed him anyway.

They walked side by side away from the carnage, and Max began to feel better.

There was the whole day ahead of them. The whole day to move the bodies. It wasn't like he was skirting his duties. After all, he usually worked harder and longer than anyone else.

"It's crazy that Dan ended up here in the end," said Mandy.

"Yeah," said Max, speaking in an absent-minded kind of way. "I gave him the directions, though. So it's not totally surprising. He's a resourceful kid."

"Seems like one," said Mandy. "It's too bad about his friend... But are you worried at all about having two more mouths to feed?"

Max shrugged. "More labor too," he said. "It'll be OK. It'll work out."

"What's going on with you, Max? You seem different. What's on your mind?"

Max paused and so did Mandy. They were standing in the middle of a small clearing where the wild grasses blew gently in the breeze. The sun was coming up and already starting to warm the air and the earth, if only slightly.

"Nothing," said Max, turning again to look at Mandy. "It's just that..."

"What?"

"After everything we've been through, I finally don't feel anything at all. After yesterday, I mean."

"You're in a state of shock," said Mandy. "It's normal."

"No, it's not that."

"Then what is it?"

"I've lost the sense that everything's going to work out."

"You've lost your sense of hope?"

"No," said Max, speaking the words with a sense of finality. "I haven't lost that at all. I don't know what's going to happen. None of us do."

"You mean with the mob? That they could come back?"

"I think that must have been the last of the big groups in this area," said Max. "The rest will have starved by now. I can't imagine how they'd managed to stay alive up until yesterday as it was."

"So what are you getting at?"

Mandy looked at him with an expression of slight annoyance, as if she really wanted him to spit it out once and for all.

But it wasn't as if Max knew much more than she did. He didn't have a crystal ball, and he didn't know what the future held. He could make guesses and he could plan. But there was no certainty in anything.

"You think we're going to make it?" said Mandy, breaking the silence of her own unanswered question.

"Yeah," said Max. "I think we're going to make it."

And it was the truth.

The two of them fell into silence as they gazed off into the woods. Spring wasn't far away, and the new season would transform the landscape.

"You ever think of having kids?" said Max, breaking the silence and looking over at Mandy.

Mandy blushed and smiled at him.

"We've got to start rebuilding the world somehow," said Max.

"I guess that's about as much romance as I'm going to get from you."

"You never know," said Max. "Spring's on the way, after all."

"Come on, let's get some coffee and get to work. Or Georgia will have our heads."

Max put his arm around Mandy's back and they walked side by side back towards the camp.

* * *

SIGN UP for my newsletter to hear about my new releases. You'll also receive a free short story, *Surviving the Crash*. http://eepurl.com/c8UeN5

ABOUT RYAN WESTFIELD

Ryan Westfield is an author of post-apocalyptic survival thrillers. He's always had an interest in "being prepared," and spends time wondering what that really means. When he's not writing and reading, he enjoys being outdoors.

Contact Ryan at ryanwestfieldauthor@gmail.com